My Precious Gift

Middlemarch Shifters 16

Shelley Munro

My Precious Gift

Copyright © 2022 by Shelley Munro

Print ISBN: 978-1-99-115877-2
Digital ISBN: 978-1-99-115871-0

Editor: Evil Eye Editing

Cover: Kim Killion, The Killion Group

This book is a work of fiction. The names, characters, places, and incidents are products of the writer's imagination or have been used fictitiously and are not to be construed as real. Any resemblance to persons, living or dead, actual events, locales, or organizations is entirely coincidental.

All rights reserved. No portion of this book may be reproduced, scanned, or distributed in any manner without prior written permission from the author, except in the case of a brief quotation embodied in critical articles and reviews.

Munro Press, New Zealand.

First Munro Press electronic publication February 2022

First Munro Press print publication August 2022

To Paul and Robyn.
I appreciate your company, encouragement, and support—for both the ups and downs of this crazy writing expedition.

Introduction

Wrap the gift in love...

When Isabella found her forever mate in shifter Leo Mitchell, she shoved aside memories of her feckless parents and her past. Her inability to have children was more challenging, but she stashed those emotions, too. That's until someone leaves a kid in a basket, right on their doorstep...

Leo adores his strong, bad-ass woman, and when the mystery behind their Christmas keepsake creates danger for the small town of Middlemarch, he isn't about to fail his mate. Together, they'll fight this hidden threat while adjusting to life with an active child. The boy might bring them even closer—if they survive the experience.

Reader advisory: this stand-alone series romance features oodles of shapeshifters, seasonal festivities and rituals, family life in a small rural town, an adorable kitten keen on Christmas tree baubles, and a puppy. Oh, and sweet, steamy loving between mates. What's not to like?

Chapter 1

Premonition

Since childhood, Isabella Mitchell had survived by her instincts. Now happily married to Leo, those days were far behind her, but her sixth sense remained. Right now, intuition screamed at her to check her incoming messages—the ones relating to her assassin-for-hire past.

She sat up in bed, issuing a hard sigh of displeasure.

Leo rolled over, his black hair delightfully tousled and his green eyes sleepy. "What's wrong?"

"I need to visit the lockup." Shorthand code for the place where she stored her old life's remnants. Leo understood and accepted the past might leap from the shadows. Not that his tolerance made the truth more straightforward. Isabella hated that she might attract trouble for her beloved mate, his brothers, and their friends.

Leo shot upright, his features marred by a slight frown. The cream covers puddled to his lap, baring his muscular chest. "What's the problem?"

It was her turn to scowl. "I don't know. My gut is telling me to check my messages."

Leo gave a decisive nod. "Right. I'll make coffee while you shower." He climbed from the bed, unconcerned with his nudity in the way of most shifters.

Isabella's unease cleared as she admired his packed muscle and his fluid strides across the thick heather-gray carpet. Her husband was a black leopard shifter, and it showed in his prowling gait and alertness, his ability to act with decisiveness. "We have time for toast," she called as he disappeared.

"You make the toast while I shower," he shot back.

"Deal," she replied, humor filling the single word.

Their fourth anniversary wasn't far away, and she loved Leo more with each passing day. Thanks to Leo, his siblings, and their wives, she'd found a secure home, a family, and she'd never been happier. The only blight was her inability to have children since chameleon shifters only conceived with their kind. She'd told Leo she was a chameleon shifter once they'd started falling in love and confessed she'd never bear a child with him. He'd assured her this wasn't important.

It'd been *her* he'd wanted.

Isabella padded into the en suite, the cream tiles cool beneath her bare feet. She gathered her long blonde hair into a knot and stepped under the warm water an instant after she turned the mixer tap in the walk-in shower. Soon, an orange scent wafted around her, and the heat of the water eased the tension in her shoulders.

By the time she entered the kitchen, dressed and more alert, the aroma of coffee filled the air, and a jaunty Christmas carol poured from the Bluetooth speaker, the volume on low. She accepted the mug Leo handed her and plopped onto a barstool at the breakfast bar to take the first sip.

For an instant, she gave silent thanks, as she always did. From the moment she, Tomasine, and Sylvie had arrived in Middlemarch, their lives had changed. Instead of weapons, fighting, and dangerous adventure, Isabella—in her teen guise—had gone to school, made friends, and learned ordinary things. Domestic things. Activities such as sewing and knitting and cooking. Once she'd taken her true Isabella form and become Leo's mate, she'd thrown herself into community events and used her self-defense and fitness skills to teach others. Her organizational abilities had aided her new friends. She'd helped herself.

Isabella surveyed the white-speckled countertops and the silver-and-bronze toaster and kettle, the gleaming glass cooktop, the stainless steel fridge, the sleek blinds at the kitchen windows and smiled with satisfaction. *Contentment.* Right now, bursts of tasteful decorations in red, green, and white and a miniature Christmas tree on the counter added to the festive spirit.

The shower turned off in the bedroom, jolting Isabella from her thoughts. Toast. *Right.* The marriage thing. Isabella retrieved the loaf of three-grain bread from the fridge, the butter, the jam, and Leo's favorite—vegemite—and set them out. Hurriedly, she popped four slices of bread into the toaster and sat to drink more of her coffee.

The truth.

Her past bothered her, specifically when it intruded on her present. She'd willingly turned her back on her profession and embraced a safer life with family and friends.

Now that she cared for Leo, enemies emerging from the muck possessed a lever to destroy her. Leo was her world. She'd never realized she could feel this deeply about another person. Marriage to Leo had completed her, strengthened her, but made her vulnerable too.

The toast popped up seconds after Leo entered the kitchen. Isabella started to rise, but he stilled her by placing his hands on her hips.

"I'll get the toast while you tell me what's on your mind and why I'm seeing that furrow between your pretty violet eyes." He smoothed aside her hair and kissed the tender skin of her neck before stalking to the toaster.

"This might be an overreaction." She fell silent.

Leo placed a plate in front of her. "Isabella, you're usually right. Your instincts are always spot on."

"I'm worried you or one of your brothers or sisters-in-law will get hurt, and it will be my fault," Isabella blurted.

Leo took the barstool beside her and reached for the soft butter and the jar of vegemite. "Isabella, none of us would even think that let alone accuse you of carelessness with security. We're a community of black leopard shifters with a few lions, tigers, and wolves sprinkled into the mix. Danger is a common thread in our town, but we have excellent systems in place for every contingency."

"But it's almost Christmas. It's my favorite time of the year. I don't want it spoiled with trouble." She risked a glance at her husband. "Stop laughing at me."

Leo crunched on a triangle of toast and sipped his coffee. "Let's finish our snack and head to your lockup. We'll face this trouble head-on and kick it in the butt."

Leo pulled on his helmet and climbed onto the bike behind Isabella. Usually, he loved whizzing through the countryside with his mate, but this morning he'd needed to work extra hard to conceal his worry. When Isabella's instincts kicked in, he'd learned to marshal the troops. Her gut was seldom wrong.

The throaty roar of the bike had two birds lifting from a pine tree branch with indignant squawks. By the time they'd finished their scolding, Leo and Isabella had whizzed beneath and were halfway down the gravel road. The wind whistled past Leo's ears, the freshness of it holding the promise of a long, hot summer. Idly, he cataloged the various scents: the dried stalks in the neighboring paddock, the summer flowers, the sunburned soil. Meanwhile, the closer they came to Isabella's lockup, the greater the ball of apprehension swirling in his stomach grew.

Isabella guided the bike along a hidden lane near a hay shed and stopped beside a sturdy brick shed. The shiny padlock on the door of the windowless building glinted in the dawn light. Isabella coasted to a standstill, and Leo climbed off the back of the bike. An instant later, silence. Leo sensed the tension emanating from his wife.

Maybe she'd find nothing amiss, and they could move on with their Christmas preparations. Both he and Isabella had volunteered to design a float for the town Christmas parade next week.

They could focus on Christmas festivities and shove this false alarm behind them.

Not an ounce of his trepidation dissipated.

Silently, he waited for Isabella to check her security protocols and unlock the shed. The building was tucked away in a valley, behind a stand of soldier-straight white pine, and most Middlemarch residents didn't know of its presence.

Apparently satisfied, Isabella switched on two portable lamps to illuminate the dark interior. Leo waited in the doorway and watched his wife scan everything with her usual thoroughness.

"Okay?" he asked finally.

"Everything is how I left it."

Leo relaxed, but a glance showed Isabella was still on edge.

"I'll check for messages. Perhaps someone hasn't heard of my retirement and has requested me to do a job."

Leo bit back his instinctive retort because right now, his input wouldn't be helpful. Isabella honestly didn't wish to return to her old occupation.

Isabella plugged her computer into a portable power bank and waited for it to boot up. Leo leaned against the nearest wall while Isabella's fingers flew over the keyboard. She muttered under her breath before jerking upright.

Leo straightened. "What is it? A job?"

"No." Isabella turned toward him, her features expressionless, although he sensed her inner turmoil. "Jaycee Howard has sent me a message. I worked a few jobs with her, and we became friends." She shrugged, her curl of lips sharp with irony. "As close as assassins can become. Trust never sits easy when you make your money killing others."

"What does this Jaycee want?"

"She wants to meet. To catch up, according to this." This time, Isabella let her unhappiness show. "She must've done her research because she knows I live in Middlemarch."

"How?" Leo asked, his voice sharp because the implications were clear. If one person had found Isabella, others might follow. "Do you think it's a trap?"

"Jaycee has a gift for tracking. I don't know how she does it, but her skill is unsurpassed."

"Is she a paranormal?"

"She acts and behaves like a regular human, apart from this uncanny tracking gift of hers. I always wondered if she has fae in her bloodline."

"Is this an unusual request? When did she send her message?" Leo asked.

"No, we've met in the past." Isabella turned back to the message on the private forum. "She has sent three messages. The first last month while the third arrived this morning."

"How do you want to handle this?" Leo glimpsed a diffidence in his wife. Unusual for a woman who never hesitated in her decision-making. Seldom did she agonize over her choices. She acted in the moment, stepping forward with confidence.

"Is there something else you're not telling me?" Leo asked, keeping his tone even.

"Yes!" The word exploded from her seconds before she began pacing.

She did one compact circle of her lockup interior and started on another before Leo grasped her arm to drag her to a halt.

Leo turned her to face him and placed his hands on her shoulders. Her gaze—more violet than blue today—lifted to his, and his heart twisted. God, he loved his woman so much. "Isabella, you're worrying me. Please talk."

"What if I bring trouble to Middlemarch? People I care about might get hurt in the crossfire."

Emotion and concern shaded Isabella's features, and everything in Leo softened.

"Sweetheart, remember you're not alone. You have my family, and I'm honored to stand by your side. Right, what will happen if you ignore the message?"

"Jaycee is an expert tracker. She'll find me."

The certainty in Isabella's voice told Leo she'd considered ignoring this message and had rejected the idea, but one thing gave him heart. He'd jerked his unflappable wife from her brief panic.

"All right. If Jaycee wants to visit, send her a message and get her to meet you in a public place. How about the café? Suggest a meeting at Storm in a Teacup. We can get Saber to have morning tea or lunch at another table. I'll sit with him, and we'll listen to the conversation. Emily will reserve a table if you ask."

Isabella nodded, but her forehead still furrowed. "I'm not sure. Jaycee is a professional and naturally wary. And what if Saber disagrees? He might be your brother, but he's part of the Feline Council."

Chapter 2

The Meet

Isabella sat at a table with a view of the garden and outdoor seating. She'd chosen a chair that placed her back to the wall and with visibility of the front entrance.

The café shrieked Christmas with a real pine tree in the corner, its decorations handmade by the local kids during an early December craft class. Christmas music poured from concealed speakers, an oldie but a goodie about holly and ivy playing at present. Each table bore a Christmas-inspired centerpiece, and several potted poinsettias decorated the cabinets.

Leo had claimed a nearby table with Saber, his older brother. Saber resembled Leo with his Mitchell black hair and grass-green eyes and was a fraction taller. Isabella didn't glance at them, nor did they pay any attention to her. Isabella was just glad Saber had agreed to her proposal. She expected Jaycee had already checked out the café and would watch the comings and goings and assess safety before entering.

A glance at her watch brought a scowl. Jaycee was officially late, which was unusual for her. How long should she wait before moving to the next step in her plan, which was hunting down her friend and demanding answers?

Footsteps sounded outside, and a tall, thin woman hobbled into the café. She paused on the threshold to scan the customers. Her gaze settled on Isabella, and she wove through the tables and customers. Shock kicked Isabella in the gut, stealing her breath for an instant. She kept her expression impassive, apart from the welcoming smile pinned to her lips.

"Jaycee," she said when her friend pulled out the chair opposite and sat. Shock hit her anew since Jaycee had aged, her face lined and haggard and, even worse, she'd taken a seat with no visibility of the café entrance.

"Isabella," Jaycee replied, her brown gaze slicing and dicing. "You're looking well."

Isabella opened her mouth and closed it again because she couldn't say the same of her friend. Strands of silver interspersed with black in the jaw length cut. Deep blue shadows beneath her eyes told of sleepless nights, and she'd lost her bountiful curves and upright posture.

Aware of the growing silence, Isabella forced a smile. "Why don't we order? I eat here often, and everything is delicious." She picked up the menu and studied it even though she knew the contents by heart.

"Just tea for me. I ate a late breakfast." Jaycee ignored the menu.

Isabella got the sense she was lying, and it raised her warning antenna. "We need to order at the counter. Is English breakfast tea okay for you?"

"Yes. Thank you."

Isabella jumped to her feet. With her thoughts racing, she strode to the counter where Emily waited to serve her. They'd decided Jaycee might recognize Tomasine, so she'd stay in the kitchen during the visit instead of working the front.

"We'll have a pot of English breakfast tea, two cheese scones, and a black coffee," Isabella said.

"I'll bring them over for you." Emily's grin turned cheeky, her brown eyes twinkling. After her recent haircut and golden highlights, she was a picture of health and a massive contrast to Jaycee.

"Thanks." Isabella didn't argue with her sister-in-law. Emily's features blazed with curiosity, and it was obvious she intended to scrutinize Jaycee at close quarters, even though Saber had ordered his mate to keep her distance.

Isabella returned to her seat. "It seems ages since I've seen you. How long has it been?"

Jaycee managed a faint smile, but Isabella didn't miss the beads of sweat on her forehead. "At least five, maybe six years since I saw you last. It was at the tiny village in Jordan where we arranged a meet. The food was crap, but the mint tea was excellent."

Memories of that day jumped to prominence, and Isabella grinned even though she badly wanted to demand why Jaycee had sought her out. "That was so long ago. I'm retired, and my life is different now."

"What made you pick this town? It's at the bottom of the world." Jaycee's lips curled in disdain.

Isabella recalled Jaycee had liked to party, and her social life was hectic. "I enjoy living here. The people are nice."

"You're married." Jaycee's gaze drifted to her left hand and her wedding band.

"I am."

Jaycee lowered her voice. "You're never returning to assassin work?"

"No," Isabella said. "Although if trouble ever walks into this town, I won't ignore it."

Jaycee inclined her head, and there might've been approval in her expression. "I haven't worked much recently. Took a break after a tough assignment."

Isabella hesitated before deciding she needed to acquire information. "Are you retiring too?"

"No. I've been sick. A tropical bug I caught in Africa that knocked me." She met Isabella's gaze, her smile wry. "You don't realize how much you take your health and fitness for granted until your body fails you."

"But you're better now." Isabella experienced an urge to edge away in case whatever Jaycee had was contagious. She had to focus hard not to betray her instincts.

"I am," Jaycee said. "The doctor assured me I'm well past the contagious stage. I completed an easy tracking job last week, and not one of my fellow contractors caught anything from me."

Isabella brushed a strand of hair off her cheek, unhappy Jaycee had picked up on her internal reaction so easily. All this happiness and finding friends in Middlemarch had turned her soft.

Luckily, Emily arrived with their tea and coffee and the cheese scones. Her friend scanned Jaycee's face, her smile faltering before she switched on her sunny attitude again. Jaycee didn't even glance at her, reaching instead for the milk jug. Isabella inhaled and relished the savory, cheesy goodness of her snack. Emily made the best scones.

Once Emily left, Isabella asked, "Don't you prefer to work in the Northern hemisphere?"

"This job was a favor to a friend." Jaycee's tone had hardened, and Isabella shot her a sharp glance, her gut uneasy again.

"Do I know this friend?"

"No, I met him after you left Africa," Jaycee said without hesitation. "We worked together and hit it off."

Isabella's frayed distrust smoothed over since truth rang in Jaycee. This visit wasn't about Isabella or someone hunting Tomasine again. It wasn't about betrayal. "Do you have another job, or will you relax until you regain full strength?"

"I might go home for Christmas since I don't have another job until early January, but since I was down this way figured I'd say hello. Don't know when I'll get down here again."

"You're heading back to Syria?" Isabella asked, startled by the answer. Syria wasn't the safest place these days, with civil war causing havoc in the country.

"No, not Syria. Most of my family is in Santorini in Greece."

"Ah, sunshine and excellent food," Isabella said, racking her brain. Had Jaycee mentioned Greece before? "I have fond memories of Crete. Remember the week layover we had there?"

Jaycee chortled at the shared memory of muscular Greek males, ouzo, and sunny beaches. "Well, I intend to lie out in the sun and let my grandmother ply me with delicious food. I don't even care if she tries to matchmake while I'm there. The chance to rest and relax is worth the aggravation."

"Winter sunshine," Isabella mused.

"Exactly."

Jaycee drank her tea but refused the scone Isabella offered to share with her.

"Where are you heading after here? And how did you find me? Was I that easy to track down?"

Jaycee laughed, the sound rich with amusement. "I am an excellent tracker. The best."

Isabella released a snort. "With a large ego."

"True, but few can match my skills. You're safe enough here in your tiny town," she added and glanced around, the seasonal decorations catching her attention. "Do they go all out for Christmas?"

"Yes, and for other holidays, too. We're having a Christmas parade later this week, and Santa is coming for the children. The week after, we have a children's Christmas party, and I have to help Emily, the lady who owns this café, make a hundred cupcakes."

"I didn't realize you were so domesticated." Jaycee sipped her tea. "Do you have children?"

Isabella shook her head. "I can't have children."

"Oh." Jaycee's expression turned serious. "Is that a problem for you or your husband?"

"Leo knew before we married. We've discussed adoption, but if we feel the need for children, we hang out with nieces or nephews."

Jaycee cocked her head, a trace of curiosity digging into her features. "But you wanted children?"

Annoyed with her friend's prying, she smiled but suspected it appeared strained. "I've always known I couldn't have children, so it's a moot point."

Jaycee drank more of her tea, appearing to take the hint and back off. "Do you regret retiring? The lack of excitement? High danger work is addictive. After taking time off, I long for the adrenaline burst of a challenging job."

"I don't miss people shooting at me or the atrocities I witnessed. In the past, I always thought I'd die doing the job. Meeting my husband changed everything. I find joy in everyday things. Christmas parades and decorations for the children's Christmas party. Wrapping presents and trimming trees. Putting up lights and making Christmas cookies." Isabella popped a piece of cheese scone into her mouth. "The town's residents are decent and caring. Friendly."

Jaycee wrinkled her nose. "Middlemarch is in the middle of nowhere. I couldn't live here. Give me a cityscape any time. This place is way too isolated."

The exact reason Isabella and Leo loved it so much, as did their friends and family. The remote land allowed them privacy in which to shift and run, to indulge their animal natures.

Middlemarch was perfect.

"What else do you do? I can't see you slipping into the role of housewife."

"Lots of different things. I run fitness and self-defense classes. Sometimes, I help in this café, and I have another friend who works at a sheep station. She loves to sew, and I sell her garments at the local markets. Our town council is active, and they organize different functions that require volunteers."

"Like what?" Jaycee leaned forward a fraction, and her eagerness surprised Isabella.

"We had a haunted house for Halloween, which was heaps of fun. I dressed as a ghost and jumped out at people to scare them. Last month, I held a self-defense class for teens. We've had a zombie run in the past, and we still hold our annual Singles ball. Emily ran a cupcake-making course a few weeks ago, and I helped with that."

"You're a terrible cook," Jaycee said with a chortle.

"Emily is an excellent teacher. My skills have improved one hundred percent."

Jaycee continued to grin, showing a shadow of her former impishness. "I'll take your word for it."

"It's a pity this is a fleeting visit. I'd prove it to you and make you eat your words along with a meal I prepared."

Jaycee issued a sigh. "Maybe another time. I should get going. My flight leaves Dunedin this evening, and I want to go shopping before I head offshore. Are you doing anything special this afternoon? I know it's nosy, but I've never coupled you with domesticity before." She laughed, and her brown eyes held an inkling of humor before her smile faded.

"I offered to help Emily make cookies and frost them, and this afternoon, Leo and I are getting our Christmas tree. We'll decorate it after dinner."

Jaycee's expression was almost wistful. "You know, I don't recall the last time I helped to decorate a tree. It must've been when I was a child.

I used to help my grandma wrap her presents. She'd make jars of jam and preserves, and we'd decorate the jars and distribute them to neighbors and friends."

"In Greece?" Isabella asked.

"No, my mother's mother. She was English."

"I didn't know that," Isabella said, surprised by the revelation. "Did you spend time in England?"

"My father was in the army, so we moved a lot."

Isabella hadn't known that of Jaycee, but then life as an assassin reminded her of an iceberg. Most of the truth lay far beneath the surface. It wasn't a profession where you made friends because trust was hard. It was the nature of the beast, with assassins playing on different sides from one week to the next.

That was one part of the business she'd hated and the main reason she'd started working alone. A betrayal had scarred her, and she had decided that one mistake was all she'd allow herself.

Working alone had been the best decision she'd ever made. She'd run across Tomasine and Sylvie and helped them survive Tomasine's nutcase husband and his family. Yep, the best decision since, through Tomasine, she'd met the Mitchell family. *Leo.*

Jaycee glanced at her expensive Cartier and rose. "I'd better go."

Jaycee wrapped Isabella in a hug. Surprised by the physical display, Isabella hugged her back but tempered her strength because of her friend's fragility. She was too thin, although Isabella bit back her concern.

When Jaycee stepped back, she smiled. "It was so nice seeing you. I might have teased you, but it's obvious you're thriving in your new life. I'm happy for you."

"Don't be a stranger." Isabella meant it even though Jaycee's sudden arrival had spooked her. "Contact me beforehand."

Jaycee nodded, but something fleeting in her expression gave Isabella the impression she wouldn't see her friend again.

"Stay safe. Stay happy," Jaycee instructed and left the café.

Isabella watched her slide into a silver-gray rental car and drive away without a backward glance. Isabella joined Leo and Saber at their table. "She seemed genuine, but she looks terrible. You heard her tell me she has been sick and intends to join her family for Christmas."

Saber regarded her with a steady gaze. Her brother-in-law was a more rugged version of Leo.

"Do you think she means to cause trouble for you? For the community?"

Isabella considered this and relaxed. "I didn't get that vibe from her."

Saber rubbed his jaw. "We'll keep a close eye on visitors to the area during the next week, just in case, but you're right."

"Well, on that note, I'd better help Emily in the kitchen. See you later," she said with a wave and hustled off to find her sister-in-law.

While she worked on rolling cookie dough, Isabella's mind kept darting to Jaycee. What she'd told Saber and Leo had been true. She had sensed nothing to alarm her during her chat with Jaycee. No danger. No ulterior motives on Jaycee's part, yet something still nagged her. What sizzled through her wasn't menace. It was something else, and damn if she could pinpoint the looming hazard.

Chapter 3

Festive Graffiti

Due to work commitments, Isabella and Leo had delayed getting their tree until the weekend. They set off early in the morning and stopped to pick up Tomasine and Sylvie.

"Uncle Leo!" Sylvie shouted when she slid into the rear of the farm vehicle. "I hope you have plenty of room for a gigantic tree." She stood a head taller than her petite mother, her skin a rich honey color, and she wore her long, curly black hair in a knot atop her head in deference to the heat.

Leo chuckled. "I've talked to Felix. He gave me strict instructions not to let you pick the tree."

"Mum will side with me," Sylvie declared, tossing her head with a teenage attitude.

"Felix gave me guidelines too," Tomasine said, her tone wry as she climbed into the rear with her daughter. "Nothing over six feet."

"Then everyone agrees." Isabella waved a tape measure. "We assess before we purchase."

Tomasine pulled a face. "Boo hiss."

Isabella turned to glare at her friend and caught the quiver of her pink lips. "You're teasing me."

"A little, but the tape measure is a brilliant idea. It's easy to get confused when you see the trees together."

"Ladies, you can choose whichever tree you want, but I have the last word," Leo stated.

"Boo hiss," Isabella said, smiling even as she poked a tongue at him.

"Can we have Christmas carols?" Sylvie asked.

"You can." Leo reached forward to push a button. An instant later, the strains of 'Silent Night' flowed through the vehicle interior.

As always, Isabella enjoyed herself immensely. Leo approved the trees, and they loaded them on the back of the farm vehicle before driving back to Middlemarch. The dull morning had turned into a cloudless, sunny day. Isabella put the window down, getting a hit of pine plus the grassy fragrance coming from a hay paddock. The farmer was busy cutting the grass to make into silage for winter feed.

Once they dropped Tomasine, Sylvie, and their tree off and helped Felix to manhandle the pine inside, Isabella and Leo drove to their place.

That evening, she and Leo decorated the tree together. Leo had told her to pick whatever decorations she wanted, and she'd gone with a multi-colored tree. Tiny colored baubles dotted the tree, plus strings of lights. The colored lights flickered on and off while Christmas music played in the background. A pine scent filled their lounge, but it was a natural fragrance that she enjoyed and, combined with the fresh floral-tinted air coming through the open window, it was perfect.

"Dance with me," Leo said once they'd finished, tidied away the mess, and the lounge was pristine once more.

Isabella grinned and slid closer, her heart light with happiness. She reached up to kiss him, and he responded in kind. Their steps slowed until they swayed and lost themselves in each other. Without warning, Leo scooped her off her feet and stalked toward their bedroom.

"Excellent idea," Isabella said.

In their bedroom, he set her on her feet and unfastened the buttons of her sleeveless shirt. He dropped the garment over a chair before turning back to her, his eyes glowing with heat. Leo ran the back of one finger over the upper swell of a breast, and that tiny teasing stroke rocked Isabella as it always did. No matter how many times they made love, Isabella never tired of his touch, his focus on giving her pleasure.

"I love you, Leo. I don't tell you as much as I should." She let him see her open expression, her honesty rather than the enigmatic one she offered to strangers.

"You don't have to say the words, sweetheart. You show me every day in lots of ways, and that counts most."

Their lips met again in a sensual kiss full of erotic promise.

Everything inside Isabella softened with Leo at the center of her world. Her body hummed, craving the pleasure awaiting them. The second they parted, their remaining clothes fell away until they were naked. Leo lifted her and placed her in the middle of the mattress.

"The best part of my day is coming home to you," he whispered.

Isabella understood because Leo was her home. While she enjoyed spending time with her friends, her mate mattered most. She ran her hands over his broad shoulders, and his muscles rippled beneath her caress. His scent—wild and rich—filled her lungs, and a moan escaped her when he ran suggestive circles with his thumb over her breasts.

Her nipples prickled, stiffened, as longing rose in her.

Leo's firm touch told he intended quick with perhaps a second round of slow and tender. Fine by her.

Leo snatched another kiss before flopping over onto his back. "I want to watch you," he said, a sweet smile curling his lips.

Worked for her. Isabella straddled his hips but avoided contact with his erection. Instead, she focused on the rest of the male real estate at her disposal. She licked his flat nipples, teasing them in the way she knew he enjoyed. She kissed his face and watched his beautiful green eyes close to better appreciate the sensations she evoked in him. It took mere seconds to trail the kisses over his jaw and down his neck, where she lingered near his mating mark. She teased it with her mouth before testing the slightly raised flesh with her tongue. His entire body jolted, and he gasped.

"Isabella," he warned.

She glanced up to witness the hunger etched into his face.

Grinning but heeding his warning, she worked down his body. She nipped a pectoral muscle before skimming her fingers over his ridged abs.

Muscle packed him, and she loved to stroke and caress, to explore.

"Isabella."

This time his voice held a plea, one she answered because this teasing and touching was a double-edged sword, turning her on as much as him. Her mate could make her wet with one heated glance.

Without further fanfare, Isabella situated her body and guided his cock into position. She sank down, taking him inside her and savoring the sensual stretch of his invasion. Oh, this never got old. She lifted a fraction and took him even deeper, his cock filling her, giving her a heavy sense of satisfaction.

"Yes," Leo said. "Now, do us both a favor and move faster. Get yourself off, so I don't embarrass myself by coming too soon."

"It wouldn't matter," she said, meaning every word. Leo was a generous lover, and she tried to reciprocate in kind.

She lifted again before dropping back down and taking his entire length. She paused, enjoying the sense of fullness and the faint trembling of his body, his purring sound of approval—the feline in him showing clearly.

Leo reached up and pinched her nipple. Heat flowed from her breast and coalesced in her sex. Unable to help herself, she lifted and resettled, repeating the process several times. She wasn't quite getting the stimulation she required, so Isabella added a finger to the mix and stroked her clit while she swayed above her mate. Heat blossomed and speared into her core, this sensual dance thrilling her.

"That's it, sweetheart," Leo said.

Isabella opened her eyes and stared down at him. When had she closed her eyes? *Didn't matter.* Leo's fingers banded her hips, their strength enticing her to move faster and hurl them both into the point of no return.

She leaned down to kiss him, and he whirled their bodies, resituating them so fast she scarcely had time to blink, let alone object. Leo powered into her, his thrusts forceful. He kissed her until she was drowning in desire and racing toward orgasm. Hungry noises escaped her, and she lifted into each of his strokes.

Then they were there, and a thick wedge of pleasure seized her, flinging her into her climax. Leo followed seconds later with three short plunges into her before coming to rest fully embedded. Their hoarse breaths came in unison.

"Thank you," Isabella said simply, although it wasn't just for the pleasure her husband had given her. It was for everything. His support. His love. The way he'd helped during Jaycee's visit with his solid and silent presence.

Leo pressed a kiss to her forehead, his affection clear in his expression. "Are you hungry?"

"Not really," she confessed. "I just want to lie here in your arms and enjoy the togetherness."

"Then that's what we'll do," he said. "We'll have a big breakfast instead."

"Or a midnight snack when one of us wakes up starving," Isabella suggested.

"It's a plan." Leo drew her into his arms, and she took a moment to savor the closeness, the intimacy. Leo made her so happy. The next thought that slid into her mind wasn't as welcome. Jaycee had found her, and her friend's visit had appeared innocent. Admittedly, Jaycee was an expert tracker, her skills surpassing most, but Isabella's brain refused to leave the subject. Had she missed an aspect when she'd covered the trail she, Tomasine, and Sylvie had left before they'd settled in Middlemarch?

The uncertainty ate at her.

What if she'd missed something? What if assassins turned up and created havoc? What if they killed

Leo or one of his brothers and their wives? Killed one of her friends?

Isabella pressed her eyes closed and swallowed hard.

"Sweetheart, what's wrong? I can hear you thinking."

"Jaycee found me."

"Ah," he said, imbibing the sound with a wealth of meaning.

"If Jaycee found me, someone else from my past might be out there, watching us now."

"Isabella, we've discussed this before. It has been years since we've had any trouble relating to you. Sure, we've had danger, but you didn't bring it to Middlemarch." His arms tightened around her. "What I'm trying to say is if misfortune is coming, we'll face it with my brothers and the feline community at our backs. We've trained for every scenario we can think of to keep the town's residents safe. We can't do anything more to protect this community."

Isabella turned to face Leo, her shifter genes allowing her to see him clearly. "But this is my fault. Jaycee came here because of me. What if the meeting wasn't friendship but something murkier?"

Leo held her gaze. "Would she stab you in the back?"

Isabella pondered the question and tested her thoughts, her reaction to the idea Jaycee might betray her. "We haven't spoken in years. Not since before Tomasine and I traveled from Australia to New Zealand."

"Is it the fact she tracked you here that's making you uneasy?"

"I'm positive I haven't made a mistake, but..." She sat up and shrugged. "I can't sleep. I thought I could, but I need to patrol."

"I'll come with you," Leo said instantly.

Everything inside Isabella softened. "Thank you, but no. You need your sleep because you have that important meeting tomorrow with the winegrowers."

"Isabella, I'm sure it will be fine. Saber and I listened to your conversation, and neither of us got any upsetting vibes. She took the opportunity to catch up since she was in New Zealand."

Isabella stood and reached for her underwear. "You should know by now I won't settle until I patrol the town."

Leo sighed. "All right. Stay safe and take your phone with you. Please, should the worst happen, let me know."

"Count on it."

Leo resettled, and Isabella continued to pull on clothes. When she reached the kitchen, she glanced down and realized she'd need to change. The buttercup-yellow T-shirt was a beacon. It showed how much she'd changed since her marriage to Leo. To be a successful assassin, one needed to blend. Buttercup-yellow was not a disguise. Sighing, she returned to their bedroom to grab a black T-shirt.

Five minutes later, she tucked a weapon into the small of her back. She slipped between the shadows, slinking from one to the next but covering the ground at a decent pace. On the main street of Middlemarch, a car idled near the pub.

Everything inside her grew tense, but she crept closer when she didn't recognize the vehicle. When she'd almost reached the older model car, three people raced around the corner of a building, their gasps interspersed with crazy laughter.

Drunk teens.

Isabella's antenna signaled with urgency, but it wasn't a high-level danger. She sighed when she identified the culprits and stepped from the shadows.

"Suzie. Edwina. What do you think you're doing?" Isabella didn't recognize the male teen with them, nor did she know the driver who sat in the vehicle, his hands clenched on the wheel. "What do you have there?"

"Nothing," Suzie said quickly, flicking her black braid over her shoulder while her green gaze refused to settle on Isabella. "We're not doing anything wrong."

"I can smell the paint," Isabella said. "Why don't I come with you so you can show me your artistic attempts?"

"You're not the boss of us." Edwina, a busty brunette, sounded remarkably like her grandmother, Valerie McClintock. Valerie was on the Feline Council, as was Suzie's grandmother, Agnes Paisley. Neither woman would approve of their granddaughters' antics.

"Yeah, we're leaving," the male teen said and brushed past Isabella.

She didn't think he was a shifter, and when she gave a surreptitious sniff, his human scent confirmed her guess. No shifter hijinks then.

"Fine." Isabella pulled out her gun.

All three teens stepped back in a non-verbal, *whoa*, their shocked faces echoing the action.

Edwina recovered first. "I'll report you to the cops."

Not what she meant at all, but she couldn't verbalize her threat in front of a human. She intended to run to her grandmother and tattle on Isabella.

"Right," Isabella said, not lowering her weapon. "We'll retrace your footsteps and see what you've been up to with your paint cans."

Suzie thrust out her chin, determination and stubbornness etched into her delicate features. "No. We're heading to our friend's party on the other side of Middlemarch. Come on, Ricky. Let's go." She clasped the teen's hand and tugged him away from Edwina.

Edwina's glare told Isabella both girls had a crush on this human. The urge to laugh backed up in her throat, but she remained impassive.

"No," Isabella said. "First, you're going to show me what you've done, and then, I'm going to watch while you clean up whatever mess you've made."

Suzie snorted. "Make us. I bet your gun isn't loaded." She darted forward, making a run for the vehicle.

Isabella didn't hesitate. She lifted her gun and fired. The shot landed where she aimed it. Wide, but enough of a warning for Suzie to realize she meant business.

The explosive pop had Suzie skidding to a halt. She retreated in rapid steps, her eyes big rounds of surprise. "You shot at me!"

"Yes, I did," Isabella said, amused despite herself. "If one carries a weapon, you should be capable and willing to use it."

"Not to shoot at people," Ricky snapped.

Edwina glared. "We have done nothing wrong."

"Then why won't you tell me what you were doing? My assumption is you're responsible for the graffiti we've had around the town over the last month."

Suzie snorted. "You can't shoot us."

Edwina folded her arms across her chest. "Yeah. You won't hurt us."

"But you're not positive, are you?" Isabella hated the smug arrogance coming from the girl. Coming to a quick decision, she pulled out her phone and hit speed dial for Charlie, a local cop.

"Charlie McKenzie." He sounded groggy and still half asleep.

"It's Isabella Mitchell here. I was walking and discovered a group of teens armed with spray paint cans."

"You know who the kids are?" Charlie asked, sounding more alert. "The Feline Council has been after Laura and me to catch the culprits."

"Yes, I have them at gunpoint right now," Isabella said sweetly. "We're close to the pub on the side street. You should hurry because they're pissing me

MY PRECIOUS GIFT

off." She hung up to Charlie's curse and bared her teeth at the teens again. "Do you see what I did there? I used honesty even if it might get me into trouble with the police."

"I'm not staying here," Edwina said. "You won't shoot me."

Isabella fired, the bullet whizzing inches to the right of Edwina. The girl released a catlike screech.

"Edwina." Suzie's voice was louder than usual and full of warning.

A car sounded in the distance, and seconds later, a siren sounded. A police siren.

Isabella grinned. Wow, she must've put a bomb under Charlie. Shooting her gun had made her angst fade. She'd sort this and patrol the rest of the town, though. Doing a thorough job would help her sleep.

The oncoming car braked, and the siren cut off abruptly.

Laura, Middlemarch's other cop, appeared, her oval face pale in the darkness, her brown-red hair in a loose halo that told Isabella she'd hustled. Charlie followed, his blond hair so short he didn't require a comb, but Isabella's lips quivered on noting his inside-out tee.

"Isabella," Laura said with a warning in her tone. "You can put your gun down."

"She shot at us!" Edwina accused, her confidence racing back to the fore.

"Because you were attempting to avoid the consequences of your actions," Isabella fired back. "You think because your grandmother does a lot for the town, you're going to skate free of trouble. I, on the other hand, have confessed my crime, which is slight compared to the property destruction you've caused."

"You shot at us," Suzie charged.

Isabella smiled, wide and toothy. "But I didn't aim at you, although you tempted me sorely."

"Enough." Laura scowled on identifying the two girls. "Who are you?" she asked the young male.

"Ricky Fisher," he said.

"Where do you live?" Charlie asked, pulling a notebook out of his pocket.

"Sutton Road."

"Your parents work for the Suttons?" Laura asked.

"Yes."

"Who is your friend in the car?" Laura asked.

"John Harrison," Ricky said.

"At least he was smart and didn't take off. He's loyal to his friends, too," Isabella added and made her weapon safe. "He could've driven off and left you to take the blame. I'll check on the damage."

"Right," Laura said. "I'd appreciate that. Make that gun disappear."

"I have a license."

"Doesn't matter. You can't shoot at people," Laura snapped in an undertone. "I'll need to press charges if I get a formal complaint."

"Understood." Isabella strode past the teens with a nod and ignored Edwina's low threats, pitched for Isabella's ears. The girl could mouth off all she wanted, but it wouldn't affect Isabella. The Feline Council was big on setting examples. Part of their punishment would be cleaning away the damage. The town would be extra spick and span for the Christmas celebrations.

As for Isabella—she'd known she was pushing rules when she'd pulled her gun, but those girls wouldn't have listened to her. Their grandmothers' positions on the Feline Council had made their granddaughters arrogant and headstrong. Suzie and Edwina had rammed boundaries in the past and escaped punishment because they were sly. Until now, no one had caught them in the act.

Isabella inhaled deeply to grab at the faint scent of paint. She walked confidently through the darkness, casting out her shifter senses to follow the trail. The reek grew more potent, and Isabella gasped when she turned the corner onto the main street. She hadn't come this way earlier, purposely keeping to the backstreets until she'd reached the pub.

The teens had scrawled slogans, motifs, and illustrations on building walls. They'd done each in Christmas colors—green, red, and white. A few pictures were arty, but most screamed angry juvenile, full of suppressed anger and frustration. Isabella would lay a bet the human had painted the artier ones. The closest one shouted, *Middlemarch sucked*, and raised fingers illustrated the sentiment. It was one of the politer slogans.

Emily's café, Storm in a Teacup, had fared worse than most, and it made Isabella wish she'd aimed to hit Suzie and Edwina. They were feline shifters and would've healed if she'd shot them in a leg or arm.

The vandalism would upset Emily. Saber, too, because it was an extra chore to squeeze into their day when everyone was busy with haymaking, shearing, and Christmas preparations.

Sighing, Isabella retraced her steps. Given her previous experience and expertise as an assassin, she'd helped the local cops before. Shooting at kids, though, probably didn't fit the bill. She should've restrained herself, although she couldn't be sorry.

Chapter 4

Surprise!

"What's the damage?" Laura asked when Isabella joined the two police officers.

"They've graffitied the building walls, including Storm in a Teacup."

Laura grimaced. "All the shopfronts?"

"Yes, although on the positive side, they've kept to a Christmas theme and used green, red, and white for their messages."

"Right." Laura turned a cop-glower on the quartet of teens. "We'll take them back to the station and hold them until their parents collect them. Once that's done, we'll take photos of the damage."

The two males exchanged worried glances, and one shifted from foot to foot. Suzie muttered under her breath while Edwina folded her arms over her busty chest and tossed a defiant scowl at Laura.

"It's too dark for evidence photos," Isabella said.

"Oh, didn't I mention that Charlie and I will return home to grab a few hours of sleep before we call the parents?" Laura said. "The cells are comfortable enough. Plenty of time to ponder your behavior."

"You can't do that," Edwina protested. "My grandmother—"

"Your artwork will appall your grandmother," Isabella said. "I'm sure Laura is waiting until daylight so everyone can view the results of your prank."

"You're horrid," Edwina snapped.

Isabella pouted. "You've hurt my feelings."

Behind Isabella, Charlie snorted, and Isabella spotted Laura's flash of a grin.

"Don't laugh!" Edwina snarled.

"You're a spoiled brat. Those business owners will have to spend time and money to negate the damage," Isabella said, watching the girl closely. Her expression didn't shift. "This prank shows your lack of maturity." *Like talking to a brick wall.* Isabella turned to Laura and Charlie. "Can I go?"

Charlie ushered the teens into his police car, and Laura grabbed Isabella's arm and towed her a decent distance from the kids.

"Don't pull out your gun again. *Please.* Do me this favor and make my life and Charlie's easier. As much as I have sympathy because those two girls are out of control, I don't want Agnes Paisley or

Valerie McClintock breathing down my neck and berating me because you took potshots at their precious granddaughters."

"Wait until they see the damage. That will deflate the oldies." Isabella raised her right hand in a stop motion when Laura would've continued. "I'm sorry I've caused you trouble, but I'm not apologizing for taking a potshot at those girls. They're entitled hellions, and I hope the Feline Council makes an example of them."

Laura gave an unhappy nod.

"Do you want help to take photos in the morning? It won't be a quick job."

"Thanks," Laura said. "See you then."

With a farewell wave, Isabella left the two cops with the teenagers. Once out of sight, she paused and inhaled to center herself. She'd expected her edginess to pass, but it remained, a tight ball of tension in her chest. Isabella prowled a circuit of the town, following her usual course when she patrolled her territory.

Apart from the lurid graffiti, everything appeared quiet. The colored illumination from the Christmas lights only highlighted the damage. The school classrooms hadn't escaped the tagging spree, and rude slogans sat alongside depictions of Christmas trees and seasonal baubles. Why were those two girls so angry? They'd had every opportunity, yet instead of embracing community activities, they sneered and refused to participate.

Isabella didn't understand. Middlemarch was a bustling country town, and the council had worked tirelessly to make it a place the residents could proudly call home. It didn't matter what age group a person fell into, Saber and his fellow council members made a point of organizing activities for them.

Ah, well. Not her problem.

The two girls would complain bitterly about Isabella pulling her weapon. She'd apologize if she had to, but the fact remained, the teens had committed a crime. If she hadn't chanced upon them during her patrol, they might've gotten away with their mischief.

The plus side of not having children. Kids came with a set of complications she was glad she and Leo were missing. She ignored the immediate pang in her chest.

Isabella continued her circuit, and after finding nothing alarming, she headed home. When she reached the end of their driveway, the hair lifted at her nape. Isabella froze, her senses jumping to assess the hidden danger. She slipped into the shadows, gaze sweeping the vicinity, yet nothing screamed irregular. No foreign scents alerted her to a presence.

Had Jaycee returned? Brought someone with her?

Isabella possessed sought-after skills, but she adhered to a protocol if someone wished to purchase her services. *Had adhered to a protocol before she retired.* Would someone risk approaching her directly? Killing no longer appealed. Her days now were busy and full of friends, family, and fun. She was learning new things—to play the ukulele for one. Isabella had sore fingers to prove her persistence. Even Leo told her she was improving, and the island strum was making sense to her.

Isabella shook herself. Yep, her wandering mind proved she'd retired. In the past, she'd never have allowed this slip. Jerked back, Isabella used her senses to check the vicinity.

Not a thing stirred.

No small animals or birds.

No sheep or cattle.

Nothing foreign snared her attention. Every smell—the odorous manure drifting from the paddock behind the nearby hedge, the dryness of the tussock grasses, the sunbaked earth—was all normal.

Isabella crept closer, taking care of her foot placement, and scanning the vicinity.

Something sat on the doorstep.

She halted, trying to pierce the shadows with her gaze.

A basket?

Isabella edged closer, her weapon in her hands.

The basket appeared innocuous.

It wasn't moving. Didn't make ominous sounds.

But it was unforeseen, and Isabella loathed the unexpected. A surprise between husband and wife worked for her—an impromptu outing or gift. An impulsive trip with her friends—that was okay.

This was different.

Isabella cocked her head, stymied and uncertain of what to do. A sudden yawn had her acknowledging her fatigue. She stared a moment longer.

The basket wasn't moving. She'd deal with it in the morning.

Her shoulders slumped. *No.* She'd never sleep with this mystery gnawing at her.

Isabella sighed.

Calling for Leo wasn't an option either. If danger lurked, she didn't want her husband injured. He was her life and meant everything to her, so she needed to deal with this mystery right now.

After another long pause, she straightened. She took two cautious steps until she stood close enough to touch the lidded basket. The dark weave bore wounds from extensive use, and now that Isabella was closer, she spotted a repair in the canework. A weird smell wafted to her. She tested the air and scowled, wishing she hadn't.

Ugh! That was mouth-wateringly bad.

She straightened abruptly, an answer occurring. She'd had other run-ins with Edwina and Suzie. Had they organized their friends to deliver this as a prank? Isabella's mouth firmed, and after a brief hesitation, she reached for the lid and flipped it off.

Something sprang up, and Isabella leaped back with a curse. The thing jumped at her, and Isabella fired her gun, diverting her aim at the last second because it was an animal.

Thankfully, the bullet went wide, and Isabella sank to the ground, breathing hard.

Whatever the creature was, it was as shocked and panicked as she.

The outside light flooded the area without warning, and the front door flew open to reveal Leo.

"Isabella? What the hell is going on?"

Chapter 5

Snow Leopard Kitty

Isabella gaped, her pulse racing. A cat stared back, but not the usual variety. This one had white-gray fur with black rosettes and enormous feet. Its ears were neat and rounded, while its eyes were a denim blue.

She and the cat traded stares.

"Isabella?"

"I arrived home to find a suspicious basket on the doorstep. God, Leo, I almost shot him." Her voice shook. Although she'd taken lives in the past, she'd never done it lightly, and to think she'd almost shot a defenseless kitty had her stomach roiling. She ripped her gaze from the kitten to stare at Leo. "Did you organize the kitten?"

"No." Intrigue colored Leo's expression. "He or she looks frightened."

"So would I if a crazy woman shot at me," Isabella muttered.

Leo grinned suddenly, his warm smile stealing her breath as it always did. He crouched and turned his attention to the kitten. "Hey, it's all right," he crooned.

Isabella pushed to her feet, then froze, her attention on the cat. A faint light radiated around the animal, and an instant later, a tiny, naked boy stood in its place.

His eyes were big and blue, his short hair a white-blond with darker streaks throughout. His bottom lip quivered, and a tear rolled down his pale cheek. "I want my mama."

Isabella swallowed hard, her heart twisting at the child's distress. She glanced at Leo and noted he was as mystified as her. Someone had left a shifter child on their doorstep.

"He's a snow leopard." Leo advanced slowly toward the boy. "Are you hungry?"

The child appeared to consider this before nodding.

"We'll have a sandwich and search for your mama." Leo extended his hand and waited.

Isabella held her breath while questions pummeled her brain. There were no snow leopards in Middlemarch, so the child hadn't wandered from his home. Besides, he'd been inside the basket and asleep until she'd yanked off the lid and startled him.

The child edged nearer and took Leo's hand. Isabella released her breath, relief filling her.

"Do you like hot chocolate?" Leo asked the child.

The child's brow wrinkled in concentration.

"Never mind," Leo said cheerily and led the boy inside. "We'll find something for you to eat. My name is Leo. What is your name?"

The boy cocked his head, clearly understanding, and Isabella froze, waiting to learn if he'd answer.

"Kian." The child hustled to catch up with Leo's longer steps. His voice was high and sweet.

"Well, Kian. This way to the kitchen. Are you cold?"

"No," Kian replied, gathering his confidence. He skipped at Leo's side, the pair so cute Isabella's thoughts turned mushy.

The two disappeared while Isabella focused on the basket. She approached it with a hint of distaste since the strange aroma she'd caught earlier was clearly cat scat or pee. Maybe it would yield a clue to solve Kian's mysterious appearance.

MY PRECIOUS GIFT

A worn red blanket lined the basket. Isabella removed it and shook the wool fabric free of droppings. Who left a child in a basket on someone's doorstep? Isabella scowled because even though her parents had been distant and focused on their assassin jobs instead of their child, they'd made sure she had shelter. Clothing. Food. She'd had the survival necessities, even if she hadn't experienced love and genuine caring until she'd met Tomasine.

Although she'd never told her friend this, Tomasine had saved her from going down the same cold, lonely path as Isabella's parents.

Which brought her back to the present. What kind of parent left a shifter child with strangers? Was it a coincidence she and Leo had received the basket?

Isabella went through the meager basket contents. A tiny blue T-shirt. A pair of denim shorts. Socks and sneakers. Kian hadn't worn shoes, so she'd bet he'd taken them off at the first opportunity. Most shifter kids—her included—had hated wearing shoes. She groped for memories of her childhood and grimaced.

She'd never truly been a child since her parents had trained her in the family profession as soon as she was old enough to understand instructions. One thing occurred to her. The black leopards around here rarely had their first shift until their teen years.

Isabella removed the clothing from the basket and scrutinized each piece. Someone had cut out the labels, so she couldn't even learn which country had produced the clothing.

"Well, that was a bust," she muttered and picked up the basket. A plain white envelope with her name on the front sat beneath.

Isabella Black.

She went by Mitchell now, which meant this person came from her past. A harsh sigh whooshed from her. She had brought trouble to Middlemarch. *Again.*

Isabella set the basket aside and scooped up children's clothing and the letter before heading inside. At some stage, she'd have to confess to Leo she'd pulled her gun and fired at smartarse shifter teens. She sighed again, not looking forward to the conversation, but it was one of their marriage rules.

No secrets.

Not that Laura and Charlie would keep their displeasure to themselves. Nor would the two shifter teens. They'd be reporting straight to Granny. Isabella grumbled under her breath. This was not an auspicious day.

She found Leo and Kian in the kitchen. Leo was talking and asking questions, but Kian wasn't saying much. He was concentrating on the toast and honey Leo had placed in front of him.

"Learn anything?" Leo murmured.

"A letter with my name on it."

Leo stilled in the middle of making her a coffee. "This isn't random."

"No. Let me read the letter." She opened the envelope and started to read.

Dear Isabella,

Meet Kian, my beloved son. I need you to care for him, treat him as yours, and watch him grow as I cannot.

Let me explain.

I have cancer, and although I've visited doctor after doctor, they all agree there is no cure for me. Now that I'm at the stage where my strength wanes, I needed a plan for my son.

Tracking you down wasn't easy, so you're safe from past bogymen. No one will find you in the manner I did. I am an excellent tracker, and few possess my skills, but you know that.

Anyhow, once I found you, I needed to assure myself you were still the same person you used to be. Despite your profession, you have always possessed a moral compass that many of our kind lack. I admired you because if you committed to something, you never wavered from your goal. Rumor told me you'd lost your mettle after the massacre in Africa. I never believed that, and when we met at that coffee shop so many months later, I could tell you had a personal mission. You were protective of the woman and child with you. It was easy to recognize the queen and her daughter, although I told no one I'd seen you.

More recently, it took a lot physically to meet with you, but I needed to see you in person to tell if you were happy. You were relaxed, and the town's people respect you. A lot of them smiled and offered greetings. You've made a home in Middlemarch, which is what I want for Kian.

Kian is almost four-years-old and is a snow leopard shifter. I met Gerry when I scored a tracking job. Gerry was in Brunei and part of a Gurkha unit. He...let's just say I fell hard and still miss him. It was kind of ironic that it wasn't his job that killed him, but an avalanche in his home country of Nepal. Gerry's parents died in the same avalanche. The aftermath has proved difficult, and once I discovered I had cancer, time was of the essence.

Until I met you, I didn't know about shifters. I saw you shift once into a lion. Instinct told me to keep your secret, and I'm glad I did.

The knowledge you could do this made me accept Gerry's secret more readily. As I've already indicated, I admire you and always have, so falling in love with a shifter didn't cause repercussions for me. We had almost four good years together before he died in that avalanche.

Your background makes you the perfect person to look after Kian and raise him to be the remarkable man I know he'll become.

Isabella, this is a huge favor to ask of someone, but you're a good person. Honorable and full of integrity. I am trusting you to hold Kian safe and give him the life he would've had if his mother and father still lived.

By the time you read this, I'll be on my way to Australia. I have picked out a hospice there and suspect I won't last much longer. The hospice will contact you when I die.

Please tell my boy how much I loved him, how much his father loved him. His grandparents in Nepal, too. When Kian is older, tell him stories of our past. Tell him the good stuff rather than highlighting my mistakes.

You should receive separate correspondence from me soon. Each night, for months, I've been working on a family history for Kian. I'm placing it in the cloud along with financial info and legal papers to give you guardianship of my son. Since the cancer diagnosis, I haven't worked as much, so I've gone through my savings. The hospital treatments took a sizeable chunk of my wealth, but there is a bit for Kian. I'd like to think it will pay for his education. Gerry was smart, and Kian takes after him. He's bright and curious, and fearless. Perhaps I shouldn't be telling you this. I'd hate to dissuade you from taking care of my son.

Isabella paused there, taking in the splotches on the page. Tear stains? She swallowed hard and wished Jaycee had told her this in person. Isabella considered this for a moment longer. No, she would've done something similar if she'd stood in Jaycee's shoes. While she adored her nieces and nephews and mourned her inability to have her own, Isabella would've panicked at becoming responsible for Kian.

She lifted her head and found Leo and Kian staring at her.

"What?"

"You croaked."

"What?"

"You made a croaking sound like a frog," Leo said, smiling, but curiosity shone through his affable grin. "Is there a problem?"

Heat filled her cheeks, or at least her face became decidedly warmer.

She didn't make excuses for her reaction or explain it. Leo could see for himself. "I'm almost finished reading the letter. You can read it next."

Leo nodded. "Do you want a refill?"

Isabella glanced at her cup. She hadn't even noticed she'd finished her coffee. "Please." She handed over her cup and continued with the letter.

I've thought about this long and hard, Isabella. You're strong and protective. Honest when it counts most. I only ever heard you lie during a job when this became necessary to maintain cover. Between missions, you were always straight up and blunt.

I appreciated the quality because I always knew exactly where I was with you. You're decent and have consistently demonstrated this, but living in the country has softened you in a good way. You smile more readily, and you're more open, yet I could still see your mental toughness. I wish I could've met your husband, but I assume he's an honorable man because you wouldn't settle for less.

This is an enormous gamble for my son and me, but I'm pleading with you, Isabella. After I die, Kian will have no one left who gives a damn. He's a little boy and should have someone championing him. He should have opportunities. Love. *I want you to be the person who stands in his corner and fights for him. Watch him grow into a worthy man. Give him the life he should've had if his parents were still living.*

I tried to do my best for Kian, considering this plan for months.

Would you please do this for me, Isabella? Raise my son and offer him the love he deserves. Don't coddle him, but teach him to become honest and respectable. Guide him in the way he requires, given his unique talents. Keep him safe for me.

Please, Isabella. This is my dying wish.

Jaycee.

"Isabella?" Leo crouched before her, his beautiful face full of concern.

Isabella blinked, surprised to find tears rolling down her cheeks. She swiped them away and swallowed the unpleasantly large lump in her throat. "Um, I'll just wash my face before I have toast and jam."

Leo's glance was searching, his green gaze probing. "Are you okay?"

She gave a quick nod and sprang to her feet. "I...I..." More tears flowed down her cheeks, and she fled, her hand pressed to her mouth to stifle her sobs.

In the bathroom, she washed her face and tied her blonde hair into a ponytail. Her inability to have children had never bothered her until she'd spotted Leo and fallen for him. Even as she'd flirted with him, she'd known Leo came from a large, close-knit family. He'd want a family of his own. They'd become close and made love before Isabella had told him she couldn't have children. As a chameleon shifter, she could only have offspring with another of her species. Leo had convinced her of his love, told her this didn't matter. She'd agreed, even as she'd consigned herself to the ranks of the married and childless.

Subconsciously, she'd craved a child.

She knew this now. She'd fight for Kian, but what if she failed Jaycee's request of her?

Earlier this evening, she'd fired a weapon at two teens. Granted, they'd deserved it, but this act of violence didn't depict a perfect mother. Hell, she'd shot at Kian.

Isabella wrapped her arms across her chest, gripped her shoulders, and groaned. It seemed she was now responsible for a child. What the heck did she do next?

Chapter 6

The Bacon Thief

Leo stared after his mate, his mouth turning dry. Isabella didn't cry, seldom displayed her emotions for anyone to see. Although she let down her guard with him to a certain extent, he still had to work to understand her. She tried hard—he knew this, so he cut her slack.

At the table, the child shoved the last bite of toast and honey into his mouth. He had smeared the honey over most of his face—such a cute kid with those lake-blue eyes.

Leo smiled and crossed the room. "More? Or how about a banana?"

Kian nodded. He didn't speak much, but he might be shy. Leo was used to his nieces and nephews who'd known love and stability since birth and chattered nonstop. They communicated without hesitation and were equally comfortable spending time with any Mitchell brother or family friend.

Leo grabbed a banana and peeled the fruit before handing it to Kian. His nieces liked banana pieces, while his nephews preferred the entire fruit. Leo kept his eye on the boy while he scooped up the letter his wife had been reading before she fled.

Five minutes later, he had a handle on her rocky emotions.

Her childless state hadn't bothered her, or so he'd thought. Honestly, he didn't mind. He loved Isabella, perceived faults and all. Children hadn't mattered when he had nieces and nephews with more imminent. But it was apparent Isabella still saw her sterility as a flaw. A readymade child presented in this way would knock her off her stride until she applied that magnificent brain of hers. They had a lot of love to give a child, and Kian was such a cutie. He needed them, and Leo thought that Isabella needed Kian too. As for him, he'd happily extend their family size. He'd give Isabella time to sort out her confusion, then they'd talk.

He glanced at the letter again, the last paragraph bringing a knot to his throat. Isabella's friend, Jaycee, hadn't looked well, and the acknowledgment of her cancer made sense of her appearance. His throat ached in sympathy.

Although Isabella had never mentioned Jaycee until the woman had contacted her, they'd had a friendship and as much trust as possible between two paid killers.

A loud fart interrupted Leo's musings. Kian giggled at the explosive noise, and Leo's lips twitched as he tried his hardest not to chortle his amusement and encourage the boy. This tossed him back to his childhood when he and his brothers had conducted farting competitions.

An instant later, the ripe stench struck Leo, and he took a step back before waving his hand in front of his nose. He hurried to open the windows even as he planned their next steps.

Kian would need clothes and a bed. His brothers and their wives could help in this department. He'd contact Saber anyway because the Feline Council should learn of this development and potential drama. He couldn't perceive problems, but it was best if the council got a heads-up.

When he turned back to Kian, the boy was watching him and fidgeting, no longer giggling. Ah! That was a silent signal he understood.

"Come on," Leo said. "Let's get you sorted."

Leo had dressed Kian's bottom half but hadn't bothered with a T-shirt since shifters had a higher tolerance for cold. Snow leopards had adaptations that especially equipped them to deal with frigid temperatures.

Leo led Kian down the passage, smiling at the inquisitive glances and the twitches of the boy's nose as he cataloged the unfamiliar scents in the house. He'd get a whiff of the lemon furniture polish Isabella favored and the citrus soaps and bath gels.

The perfume Isabella wore was a subtle floral with hints of citrus—something Leo associated with his mate and a scent that always followed her, no matter which form she took using her chameleon shifter powers.

Luckily, Kian understood the correct toilet procedure and was competent in doing the small things Leo's sisters-in-law trained their children to do from a young age. When he'd finished, Kian held up his hands, and approving, Leo led him to the bathroom. Jaycee had taught her son well.

On their return to the kitchen, Leo found Isabella standing at the double French doors that led out to their patio and barbecue area. While he'd been with Kian, she'd tidied away their dishes, restoring the room to the minimalist style that was so unlike Leo's brothers' homes but suited his mate's no-nonsense manner. She had a cup in hand, but Leo would've bet the coffee was barely lukewarm. She twisted to face him, her cheeks unnaturally pale and her breathing audible as if she was fighting panic.

Leo guided Kian back to the table and, once the child sat, Leo handed over another banana. With Kian settled, Leo turned his attention to his wife. "Are you okay?"

"Leo, when I was out doing my rounds—before we found Kian—I caught Edwina McClintock and Suzie Paisley with two human guys. They're responsible for the graffiti popping up around the town."

"Saber will be pleased. He thought a shifter was the guilty party, but he discovered human scents as well."

"The girls were real smartarses. They knew I couldn't do much with humans present. They'd intended to waltz off with no consequences because their grandmothers are on the Feline Council."

"What happened?" Leo narrowed his gaze on his wife, trying to understand the subtext beneath her words because it was lurking there for him to decipher. Normally, Isabella would act indignant and victorious at catching the graffiti artists. But there was something else.

"I called Charlie and told him I'd caught the kids red-handed."

"And?" Leo prompted.

"The girls decided I wasn't the boss of them, and they'd leave before the cops arrived."

Suspicions grew in Leo as he pictured the situation. "What did you do?"

"I drew my gun and told them I'd shoot if they didn't stay right where they were and wait for Charlie to arrive."

Ah, now he saw what had happened. "They called your bluff."

"Yes. I shot at them," Isabella said, her voice calm but her agitation unnatural for her.

"Did you kill them?" *No, Isabella wouldn't do that.*

"No! Believe me, I wanted to shoot them, but I fired close enough to give them a hell of a fright. I'm expecting complaints from parents and grandparents. Laura lectured me but let me come home."

Isabella peeked at Kian, then back at Leo. "How can I raise a child if I couldn't overcome the temptation to pull my gun on those two girls? Then, I almost shot Kian. Jaycee is foolish to make me responsible for Kian. *Crazy.*"

Leo saw Kian was watching them now, picking up on Isabella's distress. His blue eyes grew larger when Isabella rubbed her face with her hands and dashed away more tears.

MY PRECIOUS GIFT

"You're the perfect person to take care of Kian," Leo said. "I will stand at your side the entire time, and we'll have our family as a backup. We can do this."

"I want Mama," Kian spoke into the silence.

Isabella swallowed hard, and Leo understood the turbulent emotions coursing through his mate. Jaycee would never see Kian again.

"I think we'll visit Saber and Emily," Leo said. "Playing with other children might help Kian. We're going to need clothes and other supplies." He checked his watch. "It's not quite seven yet. I'll call Saber and tell him we need to drop by before he and Emily leave the house."

"Okay." Isabella scowled without warning. "We don't even have a car seat."

"It's a brief trip. We'll drive slowly and carefully."

Isabella gave a clipped nod. "Will I have to tell Saber about wanting to shoot Edwina and Suzie?"

"It'd be wise to preempt the terrible twosome before they distort facts."

"Plan," Isabella agreed.

"Grab the letter. I think Saber and Emily should read it," Leo said.

"Right." Isabella plucked the letter off the table.

Ten minutes afterward, they arrived at the original Mitchell homestead, where Saber, the oldest of Leo's brothers, made his home with his mate Emily and their twin girls.

Leo opened the rear door, and when a snow leopard cub jumped out and ran over to a patch of grass, he sighed. The tattered remains of Kian's trousers fluttered off his legs and dropped to the ground. He hadn't even heard the child's shift. Their first problem would be teaching Kian to keep his human form when they were out in public. A child wouldn't understand if he was used to changing at will. Leo and most Middlemarch leopard shifters had never experienced their first shift until their early teen years.

Another challenge.

He glanced at his wife and spotted her frown. This responsibility for a child scared her rigid, yet she'd do it because her friend had asked it of her. He smiled inwardly. Kian in their lives would mean other changes too. A little boy who'd lost his mother—they'd need his brothers and their families to help not only Kian but to support him and Isabella.

He opened the front door, and Kian shot past Leo and inside. He must've been hungry again because his nose took him directly to the kitchen. Leo and Isabella hurried after Kian, but Leo heard a masculine grunt of surprise before they arrived. It appeared Saber had met Kian.

When Leo burst into the country-style kitchen, he found his older brother crouched near the table, grasping Kian by his scruff. Kian held a rasher of bacon securely in his teeth.

"Where did you come from?" Saber asked, sounding faintly bemused.

Emily rounded the table, a wooden spoon in hand. "Aw, he's so cute. Such pretty blue eyes."

The nearest of their twins dropped her knife on her plate. "Mine," she declared.

Leo found his lips twitching as he stepped forward. He'd been doing a lot of that since meeting Kian. "Kian came with us."

Emily whirled and broke into a smile. "Leo. Isabella. You'll have breakfast with us. It's no trouble to cook more bacon and eggs."

"I'd like some bacon," Saber said, his tone mild while he eyed his breakfast thief and the small corner of bacon that still protruded from Kian's mouth. Kian stared at Saber with defiance and chewed on the pilfered breakfast.

Leo crouched beside his brother, smothering his amusement. "Kian, shift."

The kitten swallowed the last bite while staring from him to Saber.

"Kian." Leo maintained a patient tone because they'd tossed a lot at the child this morning. "More bacon?"

Kian squeaked, and Saber must've taken that as confirmation because he set the cub on the tiled floor.

"Shift," Leo said, this time making his voice stern. "Once you shift, we'll find clothes, and you can have bacon."

Kian stared at Leo, shifted his attention to Saber, and back to Leo.

Leo growled deep in his throat, loosening the reins on his leopard.

Kian edged back, and seconds later, his shift commenced.

Saber rolled to his feet, but Leo waited until Kian's shift had finished. He placed gentle hands on the boy's shoulders to prevent him from doing a runner. The bacon incentive mightn't stop the child from fleeing.

"Emily, do you have something for Kian to wear? He had trousers, but he shifted," Isabella said.

Emily smiled, biting back her questions and hustling away. She returned a few minutes later with a pair of shorts and a bright red T-shirt. "These belong to Tomasine's boys. She won't mind you using them."

"Come on, buddy," Leo said. "Let's get you dressed, and then you can have your bacon."

"Coffee?" Emily asked.

"Yes, please," Isabella said and narrowed her gaze on the fridge. "Are those new paintings?"

"Olivia and I drew them at school," Sophia said.

"They're...ah...colorful. I shot at Edwina and Suzie," Isabella blurted. "Will I get in huge trouble?"

His older brother blinked, reminding Leo of an old owl.

Leo bit back a grin. "I thought you'd introduce the topic slowly," he said to Isabella. "Not blurt it out."

"I have a lot to do this morning," Isabella said. "No time for niceties."

"Was anyone hurt?" Saber asked, settling back into his chair at the table.

"No. Charlie and Laura took them to the police station, along with the two human boys who'd accompanied them. I caught them with spray cans. They've graffitied most of the buildings on the main street. Emily, I'm sorry, but they've made a mess of Storm in a Teacup."

"Damn and blast," Emily muttered. "I've only just finished cleaning off the graffiti from last week. Tell me it's not bright pink."

"They stuck to a Christmas theme. Everything is green, red, and white. The paintings aren't too bad since they're festive. I think the humans did those. The slogans are nasty," Isabella said.

"Why did you shoot them?" Saber asked.

"I didn't hit them," Isabella snapped. "I aimed to miss, to frighten them. They intended to waltz away from the scene of the crime. Those girls think their grandmothers will protect them. They also used the human's presence to divert attention from themselves. Laura is angry with me. I don't think I impressed Charlie either." Isabella sucked in a breath. "I dislike those two girls. But, I understand my crime and will accept my punishment from the Feline Council."

Pride filled Leo as he helped to settle Kian at the table. His wife was one in a million, and he loved her so much.

"Thank you for telling me," Saber said. "Those teens are out of control. This won't be the first time they appear on our meeting agenda." His gaze shifted to Kian. "Tell me about this bacon thief."

Isabella produced the letter and handed it to Saber. "Read the letter. It explains everything we know. Kian is Jaycee's son, the friend I met at the café."

"Leo, watch the bacon for me," Emily said. "Isabella, you start the eggs." Orders issued, Emily glided around the table and stood behind Saber to read over his shoulder.

"Well," Saber said when they'd finished. "What will you do?"

"Keep him." Isabella never hesitated.

Leo winked at Isabella. "We'll do what Jaycee has asked of us, despite the obvious complications. No clothes. No bed. We're hoping you and Felix might lend us a few of the basics."

"Of course we will. Should I call Felix and Tomasine and ask if they can drop by?" Emily asked.

"I'll do it. Tomasine couldn't bear to part with Sylvie's baby things. They've used some for the boys, but they're older now. I'll contact them now if you take over the eggs." Isabella pulled out her phone and moved away to make the call in privacy.

"Kian," Saber said, his voice stern.

Kian released a squeak of protest, his gaze and his hand on a piece of Olivia's bacon. His mouth flattened into a determined line while he faced off with Saber.

"Daddy, he can have my bacon," Olivia said. "He's hungry, and he's scared. He wants his mama."

Leo froze, wild speculation filling him. "How do you know this, Olivia?"

"I just do," Olivia said, narrowing her clear green eyes. "Inside my head."

"Sophia, can you hear Kian?" Saber asked, an alertness about his brother that hadn't been there before.

"Olivia is making it up," Sophia declared, tossing her head and setting her ponytail swinging.

"Olivia, please ask Kian where we found him," Leo said.

The young girl turned expectantly to Kian, and after handing over a rasher of bacon, she stared at him. Finally, she turned back to Leo and her father. "He was sleeping in his basket, and you woke him up. You frightened him, and he thought you were the bad man."

"What bad man?" Emily asked.

"Don't push him," Saber said. "I'd say he's confused after everything he's been through. Olivia, please tell Kian he needs to stay in his two legs until we tell him it's all right to shift."

Olivia cocked her head as if focusing on conveying this message. Finally, she nodded. "He forgets. Mama always tells him two legs. He could only go on four legs with his daddy and inside if he asked Mama. Kian will try hard. He likes the bacon very much."

"Men adore my cooking, especially my crispy bacon." With that announcement, Emily pranced back to take over cooking duties amid laughter and good-natured insults.

Chapter 7

Tail Chomper

The phone rang, interrupting their breakfast. Emily answered, pulled a face, and handed it to Saber. "Agnes Paisley."

"I'll take it in the office." Saber grimaced. "I don't think I'm ever going to eat my bacon." He picked up his coffee mug and stalked from the kitchen.

"I'm working at the café this morning," Isabella said.

Emily let out a squawk. "Oh, my goodness. Is that the time? Olivia. Sophia. You need to get ready for school. Off you go. Clean your teeth and get your bags ready. Here are your lunch boxes. I'll drop you and the cupcakes for your class party off at school on the way to the café."

"But what about Kian?" Isabella asked. "Leo, you have your meeting at the vineyard."

A disgruntled Saber reappeared. "If you want, I'll take Kian out on the farm with me. Felix and I are mustering sheep this morning. We're working in the far paddock, so Kian can shift and run around."

"Did I hear my name mentioned?" Felix asked, entering the kitchen. He was tall and resembled his brothers, but his face was more rugged than Leo's with stubble shading his jaw, his black hair much shorter. "Tomasine took Sylvie to the bus stop and dropped the boys at school. She'll be along soon with clothes. Is this the fellow?"

Kian growled and bared his teeth.

"Kian," Leo said. "That's naughty. Stop. This is Felix, my brother."

"He stole my bacon." Saber dropped into his seat and exhaled on spotting his empty plate. "Twice."

The boy giggled, and something in Isabella loosened at the little-boy chortle.

"Can Felix read the letter?" Leo asked her.

Isabella handed the pages to Felix. "It explains everything."

Isabella sighed, her gut telling her that the following weeks would take work and patience. "Saber, am I in trouble with Agnes?"

"Although she doesn't condone your actions, she understands. According to her, she and Valerie are at their wits end with their granddaughters. She agreed with Laura that the two girls and their co-conspirators would spend the week scrubbing off the graffiti."

"Wow, I didn't expect that," Isabella said.

"No," Saber agreed. "How about you clean the graffiti off Storm in a Teacup's walls, and we'll call your debt to society paid in full?"

"Yes," Isabella agreed, happy with her punishment.

"Thanks," Saber said. "Felix and I will keep Kian with us until either you or Leo finishes with your morning plans. I'm not sure how long we'll take with the mustering. Some of those sheep are wild."

Tomasine, a petite brunette and Isabella's best friend, appeared in the doorway as comfortable in this busy, cluttered kitchen as she was in her own.

"I'm off to the café," Isabella said. "This is Kian, and we appreciate the clothes. Take this letter and read it before you drop it back to me. It explains everything. I'll be at the café this morning."

"Come for dinner," Tomasine invited. "I'm baking Christmas cookies and need help to fend off the hordes who sneak my cookie dough."

"Brilliant plan," Felix said. "Why don't I take Kian home with me after Saber and I finish mustering? He can play with my boys."

Isabella hesitated, then walked back to Kian. "Would you like to run in your kitty form?"

He studied her with his big, blue eyes, a tiny pucker of a frown on his forehead. His expression made her wonder how much he understood about his mother. A wash of emotion struck her, taking her by surprise. The backs of her eyes burned, and she swallowed to rid herself of the lump in her throat. How much mental and physical strength had it taken Jaycee to walk away from her son?

"Run?" he whispered, a tremor running through his entire body.

It took Isabella a moment to recognize his excitement. Given Jaycee's illness, her options to give Kian exercise opportunities had likely been limited. His education on how to hunt and evade discovery or traverse the mountain slopes would've ceased.

"Yes." Isabella pointed to Saber and then Felix. "These are my brothers," she said, keeping things simple for the child. "They will run with you, but you have to behave."

Kian considered each of her brothers-in-law and finally nodded.

"You listen to them, okay?" He'd be safe with Saber and Felix.

This time, Kian gave her a small smile, and a fist tightened around her heart. She might not have sought this responsibility, but he reminded her of herself. Her parents—well, the people who had provided the genetic material to produce her—shouldn't have had children. His circumstances differed because Jaycee loved her son and had made sacrifices to give him the best life she could, but Kian was alone as she'd been alone for most of her childhood. This morning, she'd had doubts, but now she decided she'd do everything to keep Kian safe and help him grow into the man and the life Jaycee wanted for her son.

Jaycee had given her a precious gift, and she would accept responsibility for Kian and nurture him.

Instinct had her pressing a quick kiss to his forehead and ruffling his dark blond hair. "Leo, will you drop me at the café, please? I have to see about this graffiti."

It turned out cleaning graffiti off walls was not her idea of fun, especially since she discovered the teens had decorated both sides of the building. At least one side was a Christmas tree, and it wasn't bad.

"Emily, what do you think about leaving the Christmas tree since it's on the outdoor seating side?" Isabella swiped the perspiration off her forehead. "If customer comments are favorable, you could have a seasonal mural in that spot." She wrinkled her nose and swatted at an annoying fly. The summer heat had brought them out in force.

"Back in a sec." Emily delivered a tray bearing a pot of tea, two cups, and two blueberry muffins. During the walk back to where Isabella stood, she gave a hip shimmy when the music changed to 'Rockin' Around the Christmas Tree.'

Isabella grinned. Emily's love for Christmas was contagious. She gestured at the artwork on the café wall. "I wondered if you should leave that there since the artist is talented. Maybe ask Laura to persuade him to complete the work for you?"

"How easy was it to clean off?"

"Not," Isabella said drily. "You'll need to repaint the wall to get rid of it entirely. I've done my best."

"Hmm." Emily tapped her chin. "Lots of small towns have mural art, and it discourages further graffiti. It's a feature to attract visitors."

"That is a fantastic idea. Whoever drew this has talent. Talk to Saber and Laura. Suggest the artist's punishment is to do wall paintings throughout the town."

The music changed to one about Rudolph, and Emily started humming. She frowned at the new artwork and nodded as if coming to a decision.

"Isabella, you're right. I'll discuss the idea with Saber tonight." She grinned suddenly, and it was an impish one full of mischief. "You can call Laura and negotiate terms with our budding artists. No payment, though. At least not for my murals. I'll spring for the paint, but that's all. Tell Laura I want a pre-plan on paper of what the artist intends to do."

Isabella groaned. "I should've shot Edwina and Suzie in the leg. At least I'd have a tad of satisfaction. They're shifters. They would've healed fast."

"*Tut-tut.*" Emily wagged her finger before trotting back into the café.

Isabella trudged over to her bucket of cleaning materials and attacked the paintwork with a scrubbing brush. While she worked, she watched the comings and goings and called greetings to regulars. She eavesdropped on conversations and was glad she had because it made her realize she had another problem. With Kian in their lives, they'd need to do the Santa Claus thing. While she didn't enjoy shopping, she and Leo could order online. They'd need to get extra supplies, anyway, since they couldn't rely on the others to provide everything Kian required.

That thought led to another. What had happened to Kian's possessions? He must've had clothes and toys. Books. Why had Jaycee behaved so secretly and left him on their doorstep? Why hadn't she talked to Isabella during her visit? Isabella pondered this while she scrubbed.

While Isabella might've rejected Jaycee's request, Isabella's gut told her there was more. Her phone pinged, and the unique tone warned her she had a message on her private computer. Another visit to her shed. Perhaps this time Jaycee would've left info telling Isabella more about the reasons behind her decision.

Isabella finished cleaning off the graffiti and took a break while she had a cool drink and called Laura. Neither Laura nor Charlie had contacted her today, so perhaps she'd escape serious trouble for firing her weapon. She used a napkin to wipe her face and sipped her glass of homemade lemonade while explaining the purpose of her call to Laura.

"Ricky Fisher is the artist. He and John are home from Otago University for the holidays," Laura said. "I'll speak to John's father. He's a lawyer, and his son's actions have upset him. I thought the father might be difficult, but from the discussions I've had with him this morning, I think he'll approve. I'll call you back after I speak to him."

"Thanks, Laura." After ending the call, Isabella drank the last of her lemonade and stretched tired muscles. It was encouraging Laura hadn't mentioned Isabella's weapon. She washed up and helped in the kitchen, loading the dishwasher and preparing salads for the lunch rush. Christmas carols played non-stop, and Isabella sang along, as did Ramsay, another feline shifter and one of Emily's holiday hires. His pleasant baritone blended with the music as he whipped up a banana cake and a decadent death-by-chocolate to sell in the café.

When Isabella finished work at four, she walked home. No one was there, so she rode the bike to her lockup and checked her messages. Jaycee had sent her a link to her cloud. When Isabella logged in, she discovered multiple files. She downloaded them to a file stick and stashed it securely in her pocket before closing down her equipment.

Leo pulled up in the driveway behind her. "Problem?" he asked.

"Jaycee sent me files. I downloaded them and will go through them here."

"Any message?"

"No." Isabella followed her husband into the house and took a moment to ogle his butt. The man still did it for her in a big way, and sometimes, she pinched herself because she found it difficult to believe she'd attracted his attention and his love.

"How did Saber and Felix go with Kian? Have you heard?"

"Not yet," Isabella said. "I'm thinking no phone call is good news. Saber and Felix have experience with children. They're better equipped to look after Kian than us."

Leo was quick to understand. "Jaycee trusted Kian to you, and I have your back. We'll muddle along, and we have dozens of helpers should we come across a thorny problem."

Isabella turned to him, regret and doubt tiptoeing closer to balance on her shoulders. "I didn't even ask if you're okay with Kian living here. It will change our lives. We need a plan instead of acting on impulse. We'll have to sort out his room and do Santa stuff and—"

"Isabella." Leo closed the distance between them and grasped her forearms. He waited until she lifted her head and met his gaze. "Kian is a child who needs us. He doesn't have anyone else in his corner. Jaycee has done her best to provide a future for him. She's counting on us, and by accepting Kian into our lives, we're granting her dying wish. How could we do anything else? Besides, I like him. He'll be good for us too."

Put that way, the obligation weighed heavy on her shoulders. Leo was right, and she had to stop her flip-flopping. Even when she was so sick, Jaycee's concern was for her son. "You're right. He's a cute kid, and I already have a soft spot for him. I guess we have a foster-son."

Leo smiled, the curve of his lips and the hot twinkle in his eyes stealing her breath. She reached up to skim his chin, his stubble rough beneath her fingertips.

"We should take advantage of Kian-free time," Isabella said.

Leo scooped her into his arms without a warning. "That is an excellent plan."

· ♥ · ♥ · ♥ · ♥ · ♥ ·

"You're late," Tomasine said when Isabella and Leo joined them on the patio. Felix and Saber held a beer and watched the meat cooking on the barbecue. Emily sat with Tomasine and waved on spotting them. Tomasine's boys played cricket with Emily's twins while Sylvie was pottering in the kitchen, doing something for dinner and humming along to Christmas carols.

It was a gorgeous summer evening, and the meaty aroma of steak and sausages drifted in their direction. *Yum.*

Tomasine handed Isabella a glass of white wine and Leo a beer.

Isabella scanned the vicinity. "Where's Kian?"

"He's asleep in the boys' room," Tomasine said. "Saber and Felix exhausted the poor kid. I checked on him five minutes ago, and he was still sleeping."

"I'm surprised he kept up with the two men," Emily said.

Saber and Felix wandered over to join them, both dropping into Cape Cod chairs.

"Thank you for looking after Kian," Isabella said.

"He enjoyed helping. He's agile, tenacious, and has an excellent nose. His tracking skills meant we rounded up several wily ewes." Saber grinned, the flash of white teeth wide and bright. "He scared Felix half to death. I've never seen him jump so high from a standing start."

"What did he do?" Leo asked.

"He stalked Felix's tail and chomped on it. Felix didn't hear him coming." Saber chuckled, the rough sound contagious. "Felix almost leaped from his skin. He let out a girly squeak too." Saber laughed again.

"Yeah. Yeah," Felix said. "You didn't think it was funny when he did it to you. Your roar was on the same level as mine, and I'm sure you jumped higher than me." His lips twitched. "I don't think my tail will recover soon. It had a kink in it."

"It did." Saber guffawed, this time laughing until tears ran down his cheeks.

"Did you tell him off?" Isabella asked.

"Saber batted him across the nose after Kian bit his tail, and that settled him. I thought he might slow us down, but he kept up and truly helped with the tracking. We normally go twice to muster the paddock, but we're only missing two or three ewes."

"When are the shearers arriving?" Leo asked. "Do you need help?"

"On Thursday," Saber said. "Tomasine, Sylvie, and Isabella are working in the shed. Emily has the food under control. She's helping at the shed now that Ramsay has arrived home. He volunteered to mind the café." He glanced at Emily. "The Feline Council is running the morning holiday program, but we need someone to collect the kids and feed them. Stop them from murdering each other until we're finished."

"I can do that," Leo volunteered. "I'm at the vineyard in the morning. Kian can come with me, and I'll pick up the other kids when the holiday activities finish."

"Let Kian go to the holiday program," Emily suggested. "It's art on Thursday, and they'll have the storytelling and singing. Socializing with other kids will help him settle."

"What if he shifts?" Isabella asked.

"Most of the kids are shifters this year, and the ladies running the program are shifters. Warn them he might shift and to watch him closely. Remind him not to shift to a kitty. He'll get there. Although I have to say, I'm glad we don't have that problem. Remember when Sylvie shifted unexpectedly, and we spent ages searching for her?" Emily said. "Once the kids reach their teens, they have a better sense of right and wrong and understand the need for secrecy."

"All right," Leo said. "That's what we'll do. When is the next day?"

"They're every morning this week," Emily said. "The sessions go from nine until twelve."

"Dinner is almost ready," Tomasine said. "Why don't you wake Kian now?"

Isabella set her wine on the outdoor coffee table and rose. "I'll do it." She knew Tomasine's house as well as her own since she'd lived here with

Tomasine and Sylvie when they'd first arrived in Middlemarch.

She pushed open the bedroom door, the squeak of the hinges making Kian stir. He sat up sleepily and rubbed his eyes.

"Are you hungry?" Isabella asked.

He nodded. "Mama?"

Isabella ached for him. This situation must confuse him because he was too young to understand illness and death. She sat on the bed.

"Mama is sick." She paused, at a loss over what to say next.

"'spice," he whispered.

Isabella started because he'd spoken little since his arrival. "Do you know what a hospice is?"

He shook his head.

"It's where sick people go to rest," she said, keeping the explanation simple.

He nodded this time.

"Are you hungry?"

In answer, he clambered down. He wore red shorts, and Isabella grabbed the tiny folded green T-shirt off the dresser.

"Let's put this on for you, and we'll visit the bathroom before we eat."

He allowed her to dress him and wash his face. The hair brushing wasn't so successful, but on the whole, they managed. He was a champ with doing his business, and Isabella relaxed once he'd washed and dried his hands.

The other children thundered past them to wash their hands, and when she and Kian arrived outside, the scents of meat, ketchup, fresh bread, and salads prodded her appetite.

"Let's get you fed." Isabella took a plastic plate from the stack on the end of the table. She grabbed bread, a sausage, a piece of steak and added a spoonful of coleslaw. Apart from Emily, who was a human, the rest of them had a meat-heavy diet. Emily was big on health, so they made a point of eating a few vegetables.

Isabella sat Kian at the table Tomasine had set up for the children.

He frowned and scanned faces, then brightened when he spotted Sylvie.

Before Isabella had time to blink, he picked up his plate and carried it over to where Sylvie sat with her meal. The table was high for him, but his tiny face was set in determination. A growl escaped him, and Sylvie grinned.

"Hey, little man. Did you want to sit by me?"

"Yes, please," he said.

Isabella hid her smile at his sudden manners. Jaycee had taught him the social niceties. Now, if only Jaycee had included an instruction manual with the files she'd placed in the cloud, everything would be fine.

Chapter 8

We've Got This

Once they arrived home, Leo took responsibility for Kian. He bathed him, dressed him in pajamas bearing an image of a cartoon lion, and brought him to Isabella, who was working in the kitchen, to say goodnight.

"Found anything?" Leo asked.

"Nothing helpful." Isabella glanced up from her laptop to see Kian stroke the lion on his yellow tee. He issued a sound resembling a purr. *So cute.* "Ready for bed?"

"Not tired."

"Oh," she said.

Leo grimaced. "We're going to watch a movie."

"Nothing too scary."

"Yep, I know the drill," Leo said. "My ears are still ringing from when Emily told me off for letting her girls watch Bambi."

Isabella snorted a laugh. She'd had the same lecture at a different time. "I enjoyed that one when I was a kid."

"As Emily pointed out, I'm a boy, and you're an assassin, plus your parents were assassins. Girls are different."

A pang of hurt ricocheted against a raw nerve. Isabella tried to brush it aside, but the pain was deep and crept out at unguarded moments. She'd never wanted to be different, hadn't chosen her parents or her occupation. Her parents had expected—*no*—ordered her participation, stripping away her innocence at a young age, which now fed her doubts about being a role model for Kian.

"What are you going to watch?" she asked, more to divert her thoughts than wanting the answer to her question.

"I don't know. Depends what I can find on the streaming services." Leo paused, his face scrunched in an adorable way that enticed her to grab him for a lusty kiss.

She half rose before sinking to her chair again with an inner sigh. Another adjustment with a kid around—no spontaneous sex in whatever room they inhabited.

"Maybe that one with the green ogre. It's got farting." He grinned at Kian. "Boys relish that stuff. It makes them laugh." He held out his hand. "Come along, little man. Let's watch a movie."

Isabella massaged her temples to rid herself of the tension headache that had made an appearance, her focus on Leo until he and Kian disappeared. Doubts continued to thump her over the head. Jaycee was mad to leave her son here. She'd pulled her gun on teenagers, for crying out loud. "And moaning about the responsibility won't make it disappear," she muttered.

She rose and drank a glass of water before applying herself to the files Jaycee had sent her, checking each one. Jaycee had named the folders and files, and the titles agreed with the contents. Most of the folders related to Kian. Some contained medical records of childhood vaccinations and illnesses. On the bonus side, Kian was a healthy wee tyke. Another contained details of his likes and dislikes for food, clothing, toys, books, and a dozen other things Isabella had never considered.

There were baby photos and several of Jaycee with a dark-haired man with a beaming smile. Her husband. Jaycee had included her medical details along with those of her husband. Financial information plus a copy of Jaycee's will and signed legal papers to give her guardianship of Kian. The Dunedin lawyer had dated them the day she had met Jaycee at the café.

Tears welled in Isabella's eyes when she read the stark words in a separate note. After her husband's death, Jaycee had moved around, searching for a place to call home. Then, she'd become sick and couldn't work. She'd eaten through her savings at an alarming rate, and she sorely regretted the woefully small amount she'd leave for her son and his future. Thankfully, the hospice didn't charge so Isabella could use the money from her online bank account for Kian's costs.

"Oh, Jaycee," Isabella murmured. She had hidden reserves she'd never touched and more than enough to provide for Kian in Jaycee's absence.

Kian was welcome to the money for his education. A salve to Isabella because here was a worthy cause for the cash she'd earned by shedding blood.

Once she'd finished, Isabella saved the files to her private cloud and locked the stick in their safe in the pantry. She made a pot of tea, added a glass of warm milk for Kian and a plate of cookies to her tray, and carried it into the lounge to join her men.

Her men. She sighed. Still no instruction manual. Men should come with guidelines to aid clueless females around the world.

Leo and Kian were watching a cartoon about lions, and the music was familiar. She set the milk in front of Kian and handed him a cookie.

"Thank you," he said, and Isabella's eyes widened. Kian was more vocal, and that had to be a good omen.

She passed Leo his mug of tea.

"Thanks," he said.

Isabella settled next to him with her tea. "How is the movie?"

"Not too bad," he said. "Emily and Tomasine took the kids when it first released. All the kids went around alternatively roaring and singing the songs for weeks afterward."

"I prefer old music," Isabella said.

"I know. You're hopelessly old-fashioned."

"No, I'm not!" The words stung. She walked out of step with so many things, and Leo pointing out her differences didn't help.

"Hey." Leo held up his hands in a signal of surrender. "Sweetheart. I love you. It was because you were an original that you grabbed my attention. Although to be fair, you chased me at first. I thought you were out to trap me."

The reminder brought a rush of memories. Leo had attracted her from the beginning, even when she was playing the part of a plump teenager. It had been Leo who set her pulse racing. All these years later, she still pinched herself because Leo was incredible.

"It's fine for you to enjoy classical music rather than pop," he said. "We should have differences and interests and hobbies in common. You enjoy helping Caroline sell her clothes at the market and playing the ukulele. You've tried lots of new things since we got together. Change is good for us." His glance at her encompassed Kian for fleeting seconds. "This recent surprise will help us grow together. Felix and Saber informed me tonight their kids are constantly throwing them challenges, and half the time, they're clueless about the right way to proceed. According to them, they muddle through, make mistakes, and improve the next time. We'll blunder too, but we'll work together to do our best."

Isabella's heart squeezed hard, and everything inside her softened.

Leo was right. They muddled through this marriage thing, constantly changing and resetting the goalposts. Adding a child to the mix was the next step, and even if they weren't ready, they'd cope.

The movie finished, and Isabella cleared away the remnants of their supper while Leo put Kian to bed.

"No." Kian dug in his heels when Leo attempted to urge him toward the spare bedroom. For an instant, her mate appeared nonplussed. Then he smiled. "How about I read you a story while you get ready to sleep?"

Isabella held her breath while Kian cocked his head, appearing to consider the suggestion.

"You'll need to lie flat on your bed and listen while I read the story." Leo dangled the bribe again, and Isabella waited for Kian's reaction.

"Long story."

"Of course," Leo agreed and urged Kian to his bedroom.

According to the notes Jaycee had left for him, Kian enjoyed the outdoors, and other animals fascinated him. Henry, one of the two werewolves who made Middlemarch their home, bred large-breed puppies as part of the Feline Council's strategy to help the shifters blend and remain safe in the human world. Dozens of families had adopted puppies that grew to one size. Massive. But this meant human residents became conditioned to seeing large animals loping in the distance, and their minds took them directly to dogs and pets. Perhaps they should ask Henry if they could visit his puppies. She'd discuss the visit with Leo once Kian was asleep.

Isabella turned off the TV. When she peeked into Kian's bedroom, Leo was still reading—something about a cat wearing a hat—although why they'd do that, Isabella had no clue. Kian enjoyed the story, though, and watched Leo with wide eyes. He didn't look as if he might go to sleep anytime soon.

She cast her mind back to when Sylvie was a child. What had Tomasine done when her daughter refused to go to sleep? She'd sung a lullaby, or when they weren't camping in the wild, she'd used an app on her phone.

Isabella hurried off to find her phone and thumbed through various apps. Finally, she settled on one with nature sounds. Kian had spent time in the mountains with his parents. If Kian hated this one, she'd try another, but he had to sleep. Ironic amusement filled her. She was the adult here, yet exhaustion made her limbs heavy while Kian appeared ready to power through the night.

A craving for sleep had her shoulders hunching and a yawn escaping, their big soft bed alluring. Isabella smothered another yawn and hustled back to Kian's bedroom.

Leo was reading yet another story, this one about green eggs.

She recalled that one, but it had never made sense either. Who wanted to eat stinky green eggs? Isabella set up the phone and waited until Leo finished the story. "It's time for you to sleep now."

"No." Kian sounded mutinous.

Possibly, they shouldn't have let him sleep so long earlier. A lesson learned for the future.

Leo closed the book and set it aside.

"More," Kian demanded.

"Tomorrow," Isabella said firmly. "One of us will read to you tomorrow. Instead of reading, you can listen to the jungle music."

Kian scrunched his forehead, but she ignored the show of temper and signaled for Leo to leave. He took the hint and disappeared.

"This is special music for nighttime." Isabella mentally crossed her fingers, praying this would work.

She pushed the start button, and the faint sounds of rustling trees, dancing grasses, and chirpy insects emerged from the speaker. The wind blew, creating gentle music, and Kian's muscles relaxed. With his shifter senses, he'd hear every insect click. A faint wolf howl sounded, and Kian grinned at her.

Isabella sighed with relief and fought another yawn. She'd had her first win as an adoptive parent, and she'd take it. "You listen to nature, okay?"

"Yes," Kian said, his eyes bright with interest.

He didn't appear in the least bit sleepy, but if he'd stay put, that was half the battle. He'd fall asleep, eventually.

"Good night." She hesitated before leaning close to him and kissing his cheek.

He didn't react, intent on listening to the app. Isabella took the hint and joined Leo in the bedroom.

"Is Kian asleep?" Leo was already in bed and reading one of his favored thrillers when she entered the en suite.

"He's listening to a nature app. I hope he'll drop off to sleep or in the future accept the sounds as a cue to sleep." Isabella washed her face, cleaned her teeth, and returned to the bedroom. "I'm tired. Kian mightn't want to sleep, but I do." She paused, trying to think like a parent instead of a confused stand-in. "Is the door locked?"

"No."

"What if Kian goes walkabout?"

"We'll track him down and bring him home." Leo yawned. "I imagine we'll hear him. You have bat ears."

Isabella shucked her clothes and slid into bed beside her husband. "Is that an insult?"

"No." He grinned over the top of his tablet. "It's an observation. Don't worry. We've got this."

Chapter 9

Christmas Tree Drama

Leo woke from a deep sleep when something bounced on his belly. A rough tongue slapped across his cheek, driving him to greater wakefulness. On opening his eyes, he came nose-to-nose with Kian in his feline form. Or rather, his butt. He'd turned to give Isabella the same wake-up treatment. Leo lifted onto his elbow and grinned as Isabella murmured a complaint.

Next, he noticed the muddy footprints on the plain silver-gray bedcovers.

Isabella had been right to suggest locking the doors. This kitty had explored the garden.

Leo reached for his phone to check the time. Six. Close enough to their usual wake-up time. He grasped Kian and turned the kitten to face him. "Are you hungry?"

Kian replied with a yowl. Good enough. Leo rose and dressed in his summer uniform of T-shirt and shorts. Then, he picked up Kian and toted the kid to his room. The nature app was still playing, and Leo turned it off.

"Shift," he ordered the boy.

Five minutes later, they were in the kitchen, and Leo was scrambling eggs. A distinct muddy trail of footprints led from the open front door and down the passage toward the bedrooms. At least Isabella's worst imaginings hadn't occurred. Kian was still here and hungry.

Isabella appeared and walked straight to the coffee machine. She shoved in a capsule and set the machine working. "Do you want coffee?"

"Please." Leo loaded four slices of bread to toast. "We should've locked the doors."

She scowled. "Yeah, I noticed the muddy footprints. I'll clear the mess later."

"What time is Tomasine coming?"

"About quarter to nine. I hope Kian doesn't decide to shift in public."

"We'll talk to him," Leo promised. "He understands, I think. We'll reinforce the rules.

Hopefully, the kids will keep busy this morning. Kian will follow their lead and stay in two legs."

Isabella's brows rose until she resembled an inquisitive fairy with her blonde curls and natural face. "Promise?"

Leo barked out a laugh. "No promises. All we can do is our best."

"I need a pep-talk," Isabella announced.

"Me too," Leo said. "I thought I'd absorbed this parenting stuff from my brothers. Turns out it's different when you have to do it yourself."

"Tell me about it." Isabella picked up the two mugs of coffee and set them on the table. "I'll collect Kian at lunch and keep him occupied in the kitchen while I help Emily. I'm sure that will be all right."

"Just don't let him sleep," Leo said. "Suggestion. Let's have a picnic dinner tonight and go somewhere we can shift and run. Tire the little man until he's ready for bed."

Isabella brightened. "Plan. We have Christmas carols the next night and other Christmas things. The parade and the children's party. We'll keep him busy."

"Excellent. We'll embrace Mitchell family Christmas rituals," Leo said. "That should do the trick."

Isabella nodded, but a doubtful expression etched into her face. "It's worth a try."

Leo laughed. "We'll get through this. All three of us."

"I hope so."

The following week was a blur of Christmas celebrations and activities ranging from cookie exchanges to parades and parties. Isabella watched Kian in her peripheral vision as Ramsay showed him how to shape cookies. The tip of Kian's tongue poked from the corner of his mouth as he fiercely concentrated on the process. They'd had a few difficulties. It was apparent he missed his mother, and she and Leo had printed a photo of Kian's parents and framed it for the child. He loved this and had smeared the glass with tiny prints since he often fell asleep with it clutched in his arms.

Isabella's heart ached for him, yet there was nothing she could do to ease the wrench of separation from his mother.

A crash in the living room had Isabella halting dinner preparations and hustling to the lounge. She steeled herself since they'd already had a few breakages. A curse escaped when sudden pain radiated from the sole of her foot. *Those damn building tiles.* This wasn't the first one she'd stood on. Isabella scooped up the bright yellow piece and shoved it in her pocket. How could one small boy strew toys and clothes so far without raising a sweat?

She arrived to find their Christmas tree on its side and angry cat yowls coming from beneath the decorated branches. Isabella bit her bottom lip. She and Leo had saved the tree from this fate already this week.

"Kian." She pushed sternness into her voice when she wanted to laugh at the panicked shudder of the tree, the rattle of the ornaments, and the increasingly flustered yelps and growls. "Hold still while I fix the tree."

The tree ceased moving, and Isabella lifted the pine off Kian.

Shiny red and silver ornaments bounced on the floor. The glittery objects must've enticed Kian because he took off, pouncing and sending them flying across the carpet. Isabella struggled to position the tree on its stand and grab an enthusiastic Kian hell-bent on capturing the shiny baubles.

"Kian!" The masculine command had Isabella and Kian freezing.

Isabella glanced over her shoulder. "Tree or Kian?"

Leo winked and darted forward to intercept Kian. "I'll take the wee cub and give him a lecture on the correct behavior around Christmas trees."

"Thank you." While the tree smelled wonderful with its pine scent, Kian's collision had caused an explosion of needles. A distinctly loud crunch beneath her foot had her groaning.

She'd smooshed a decoration into the carpet.

Isabella maneuvered the tree back into position and gave it a sharp tug to ensure it wouldn't topple again. That's if Leo's lecture sank in.

The distinct scent of burning onions filtered through her consciousness, and she yelped one of the swear words she'd tried to censor from her language since Kian's arrival. She picked her way across the carpet, dodging loose baubles, and hurried into the kitchen.

Phew! She whipped the pan off the heat, thankful that her shifter super-senses had alerted her before she charred the onions beyond saving.

Isabella left the lounge cleanup until later and returned to dinner prep. Ten minutes later, Leo strolled inside with a repentant Kian sans clothes.

"Kian is going to say sorry before he gets dressed for dinner. He is also going to help me set the dinner table." Leo winked at Isabella.

Kian shuffled and stared at his feet.

"Kian," Leo prompted.

"I am sorry for hurting the tree," the boy said, lifting his head briefly.

"And what else?" Leo asked.

"For turning kitty inside without asking."

"Good boy," Leo said.

"I haven't finished clearing the lounge," Isabella said. "Dinner needed my attention."

"Let's do it later. We've got the Christmas carols tonight." Leo led Kian from the kitchen, the pair chatting as they headed for Kian's bedroom.

He was talking more now that he was becoming used to them, but they hadn't managed to stop him from shifting from human to snow leopard and back at will. Thankfully, he didn't do it with other adults or children, but he was a terror at home. It wouldn't matter, but Leo often had staff dropping in or business meetings relating to the vineyard. Although some were online meetings, employees spotting a snow leopard racing around in the background or jumping on Leo's knee wasn't stellar.

Kian and Leo arrived back in the kitchen.

"Did Kian tell you about seeing Santa Claus at the party?" Isabella asked.

"He smelled the same as Mr. Saber," Kian said.

Leo's lips quivered, and he and Isabella shared a moment of amusement.

"Dinner is almost ready," Isabella said. "Kian, we're singing tonight."

Kian straightened, puffing out his chest. "I like to sing."

Curiosity had Isabella turning her attention from the pot of mince she was heating. "What are your favorite songs?"

"Kitty songs. They ring through the mountains with joy."

Realization struck Isabella, as did the echoes of one of Kian's parents. Kian had heard the words often and was now repeating them.

Leo crouched before Kian and made sure the boy was paying attention. "We need to sing human songs tonight. Isabella and you and me must stay in two legs to sing."

A tiny frown etched into his features. "No kitty singing?"

"No. Isabella and I will take you kitty singing another time. Okay?"

"Mama couldn't do kitty singing," Kian said.

Sadness twisted inside Isabella, and she turned away to hide the moisture in her eyes. Jaycee had lost so much, and right then, she solidified her promise to herself. She'd do her utmost to ensure

Kian grew up knowing his mother had loved him, sacrificed everything for him.

"Leo, can you make toast for me? Kian might help."

Isabella poured a glass of milk for Kian. A few minutes later, Leo handed her the toast. She buttered it and placed the slices on plates. When serving Kian's meal, Isabella plated it differently by cutting the toast into cubes and strips and turning his meal into an arty face. She added crisp potato strips to fill the hair with one or two curls of zucchini as vegetable decoys.

"No vegetables tonight?" Leo asked.

"Emily suggested I hide them, so I took her advice."

Isabella grinned at Leo's scrutiny of the mince.

"Ah," he said. "Want a glass of wine?"

"Not right now. Kian, are your hands clean?"

"We washed them before we came to help you." Leo lifted Kian onto his chair and shunted his glass of milk closer.

Kian ran through his usual pre-meal performance. He sniffed the food, drawing the scent deep into his lungs. "Face," he said. "Pretty."

Triumph suffused Isabella. She'd done a clever parent thing. She'd spoken with Emily and Ramsay and discussed mealtime problems. Both had given her suggestions to add more vegetables without Kian realizing. Ramsay had offered the hint of distraction with food art.

"Well done," Leo murmured.

The quiet words of praise thrilled Isabella more than the wins of the past when she'd taken a tough shot or completed an assignment. While this parenting gig was complex, perhaps she was up to the challenge. Emily had told her she and Saber had struggled with parenting, and she'd confessed it was the hardest thing she'd ever done. Isabella's doubts were normal.

While Isabella had listened, privately she'd decided the example her parents had offered had killed any parental genes she might've possessed. Emily and Tomasine had told her to ask if she needed advice, that no question was stupid.

"Kian and I had a chat about rules," Leo said.

Isabella watched Kian pop a piece of the green zucchini hair into his mouth and chew. He didn't spit it out. *A win!* "What rules?" she asked.

"If Kian wants to turn into a cat while he is inside, he can, but he has to ask either you or me first. We'll tell him if it's okay or if he has to stay in two legs."

"That sounds fair," Isabella said. They couldn't be inflexible because she understood the beast's craving for freedom. It must be more difficult for a child to resist the siren call.

"We need to make sure we have regular family outings," she murmured.

"Yes. I was talking to Saber earlier. We're looking into purchasing a remote parcel of land. Each of us would contribute to the purchase price. We wouldn't build on the land but would keep it as a place to embrace our cats. Camp and let the shifter kids have the freedom to be themselves. We'd want undeveloped land with water, plenty of trees, and mountains—a place where Kian could sing."

"That's a brilliant idea. We've noticed kids are hitting their first shift earlier than in the past. An isolated farm would be perfect for them to embrace their feline sides. Count me in for financial contributions."

Leo nodded. "I thought you'd say that. Saber intends to speak with Felix and the twins when he catches up with them. With the next generation here, it's time to consider this idea seriously."

"I still can't believe Joe, Sly, and Kiera are having twins."

Leo barked out a laugh. "It's poetic justice my twin brothers will have their own twins to turn their hair gray. They were hellions growing up." He paused, his grin widening. "Not that Felix and I were goody two shoes."

"I've heard Saber's tales about your lives after your uncle died. I wish I'd met your Uncle Herbert. He sounds amazing to take over raising five boys."

"We were lucky to have him. Most single men wouldn't have taken us on." Leo's smile faded. "We were also fortunate to have Saber in our lives. After Uncle Herbert died, Saber held us together as a family. It's thanks to him we have such tight bonds now. That's why I haven't hesitated to let Kian into our lives. It won't be smooth travels, but the kid deserves a chance after his rough start to life."

Isabella reached for his hand. "You're a good man, Leo Mitchell, but I sensed that from the beginning."

"You broke into my hotel room and tried to seduce me."

Isabella rolled her eyes. "Let it go, Leo. Besides, it worked, didn't it? Now, eat your dinner, or we'll be late for the Christmas carols."

Chapter 10

Kid Shenanigans

When they reached the school, picnic blankets and folding chairs studded the rugby field. Thankfully, Saber and Emily had saved a spot for them. Kian joined the girls and Tomasine's boys. Emily handed Kian a bowl of tiny meaty snacks, and he seemed happy enough sitting with the other kids.

Isabella sank onto a blanket next to Leo and cuddled against his side. She listened to the Christmas carols sung by local groups and the school choir. Some were fantastic, while other singers displayed more enthusiasm than skill. Emily handed around cups of boozy coffee, and they ate shortbread and fruit mince pies. Although Isabella had enjoyed many community nights, this one was better because of Kian. Ten times better. With a child, she experienced inclusion rather than feeling as if she stood outside a window and stared inside.

As the singing continued, she checked on Kian. He hadn't asked after his mother, although he spoke about her and his father and, occasionally, his grandparents. From what Jaycee had told her, she'd continued hiring herself out to whoever paid for her skills. Kian would be used to her long absences. Isabella frowned. What had she told him? And what would Jaycee have done if Isabella had refused Kian?

A child forced into an untenable situation or struggling to care for themselves bothered her—echoes of her past. Children required nurturing. Oh, her parents had provided for her, given her food, clothing, and shelter. She'd had material things but not their loving support.

"Isabella." Leo's whisper jerked her from unwelcome thoughts. "What's wrong? You're frowning so hard, I'm having trouble hearing this wonderful singing."

Isabella leaned closer to him. "The singing is terrible. Admit it."

"Have you received another message from the past?"

She softened inside at the caring note in Leo's voice. He never chastised her for bringing trouble to Middlemarch. Nor did Saber, although she must make life difficult for him with the rest of the Feline Council. She helped with security and community activities, but guilt still swamped her each time her past trespassed on the lives of innocents.

"Isabella?"

And she'd drifted again. "No, I was thinking about Kian. I realized he hasn't asked about Jaycee recently. Has he talked to you?"

"He hasn't asked me when she'll be coming home."

"I'm not even sure if he knows how sick she is."

"Or he might be waiting for us to mention the subject," Leo said.

"He's four. Kids, in my limited experience, blurt stuff out as it occurs to them. They're not secretive. They don't keep thoughts to themselves."

"Can you recall what you were like at Kian's age? Did you chatter?" Her shifter vision picked up the flash of white teeth in the subdued lighting.

Isabella wrinkled her nose, and his quick laughter told her he'd seen. "You could never call me a chatterer. Not even at age four. Sometimes my parents used me as a distraction during jobs or to retrieve items from places they couldn't fit."

Leo cursed under his breath. "I'm sorry, sweetheart."

"Doesn't matter. I'm more worried about Kian. Should we talk to him about his mother? Tell him she is sick and won't be coming home?"

"Let's play it by ear. Give Kian a chance to become used to us. Let's make a point of sitting together and discussing our days."

"At dinner," Isabella said.

"We could ask him what he wants Santa to bring him for Christmas."

Unexpected excitement burst through Isabella. "I've never been Santa before."

"With your shifter capabilities, you could easily shift to a Santa form." Leo's warm amusement suffused her but didn't dim her sweet anticipation. She recalled the days when she'd pretended to be a teenager, Tomasine had organized a Santa gift for her and Sylvie. The presents had been cheap and homemade, but Isabella still experienced a wash of love every time she recalled those traditions.

"All right," Isabella said. Emily and Tomasine had conferred on Santa's gifts last week, but a customer had come, and Isabella had gone to serve the woman and missed the conversation. They shouldn't overindulge Kian but give him a few small things for him to enjoy. A book. He might like crayons or color pencils. Maybe a T-shirt and a bar of chocolate.

"I wonder when Kian's birthday is? I didn't pay attention to dates. Did you?"

"Jaycee included his birth certificate with the documents in the cloud. I'll check when we get home."

"How long does this continue? The kids are getting restless," Leo said.

Saber spotted the same sly ponytail tug Leo did and tapped Felix on the shoulder. "Your boys are firing the opening salvo in a war."

Felix groaned. "They're shaping up to follow in our footsteps."

"I feel as if I should laugh," Saber muttered. "But my girls are just as naughty. I was deluding myself thinking girls would be easier."

The head teacher clapped as the song finished. "Thank you, ladies. That was splendid. We're going to end the night with the students singing 'Silent Night.' Please join in and get out those phones to shine a light on our singing."

The music started, and the vocals were noticeably less screechy when everyone sang.

Kian shuffled closer to Saber's daughter, Olivia, when Felix's youngest boy shoved him. Leo nudged Saber, and they witnessed Olivia whack Bryce.

Saber muttered under his breath. "It's home time. Let's move now before there's a general exodus."

"Are we still dropping by the café for supper?" Leo asked.

"Given our children's behavior, we should head straight home," Saber grumbled. "But they'll be all together, and I'll give them a lecture on correct behavior." He brightened. "Yeah, that should work."

A snort escaped Leo, one echoed by Felix.

"Lectures worked well for us after Uncle Herbert died," Felix said.

"I know," Saber said, "but I've got to try."

Isabella grinned because she'd noticed the scuffling between the kids. "Kian is joining in. That's good. I thought he'd be more downcast, but from what I gather, Jaycee was away a lot, especially after she received her cancer diagnosis."

Saber pounced and told the kids they were leaving. Isabella busied herself tidying away the various plastic glasses and plates they'd used. The Christmas carol ended, and everyone around them clapped and cheered.

"Thank you for coming. See you next year," the head teacher shouted.

Families packed up and walked to their cars. Cheery goodnights rang out, and tired children yawned. Isabella spotted Suzie and Edwina with their grandmothers. Edwina noticed Isabella and sneered at her before nudging Suzie. Neither girl appeared happy, and Isabella would bet the girls had attended under protest.

It was times like this when Isabella was glad of her solitary childhood.

"You organize Kian, and I'll grab our basket and blanket," Leo said.

"Kian, are you ready for a Christmas cupcake?" Isabella asked. "One with Santa on the top?"

Kian's gaze ran past her to Saber and Emily, who were shepherding their girls. He leaned closer to Isabella. "Mr. Saber is on a cake?"

A chortle emerged from Isabella, taking her by surprise. "No, you'll see." She held out her hand, and satisfaction filled her when Kian curled his fingers around hers. She matched her steps to his shorter ones, and Leo trailed behind. Not long after, they arrived at the café to join Leo's brothers and their families.

Isabella walked over to Saber after Kian ran off with the other children. "Kian is on to you," she announced. "I asked him how he liked the children's Christmas party, and he told me that Santa smelled like Mr. Saber."

Saber's mouth dropped open for an instant. "None of the other kids noticed."

"Noticed what?" Felix said.

MY PRECIOUS GIFT

Leo stepped behind Isabella and wrapped his arms around her waist. She leaned back into his warmth.

"Kian told me Santa had the same scent as Mr. Saber," Isabella repeated. "When I mentioned cupcakes with Santa on them, he seemed concerned that Mr. Saber was on the cupcakes or squashing them. I'm not sure which."

The youngest of Leo's brothers, Joe and Sly, joined them in time to hear the cupcake story. Both held plates of the Santa cupcakes to distribute. Isabella had taste-tested one earlier, and she didn't hesitate. She grabbed the closest and took a bite, savoring the hint of orange and the accompanying warm spices of cinnamon and ginger. The tiny Santa standing on top disappeared with a crunch of her teeth.

Isabella's phone rang, and she pulled away from Leo to glance at the screen. After popping the last bite of the cupcake into her mouth and chewing, she frowned, noting the Australian phone code. She swallowed before speaking. "Do you think it's Jaycee?"

"One way to find out," Leo said.

Isabella answered the call, offering a cautious, "Hello."

"Is this Isabella Mitchell?" a woman asked.

"Yes," Isabella replied.

"This is the Queen Charlotte Hospice in Melbourne. Jaycee Howard asked me to contact you when the time comes."

Isabella swallowed hard. Surely Jaycee hadn't died already? It'd been a mere two weeks since she'd left Kian on their doorstep. "Yes?" she said, the word holding a question. All her anxiety and apprehension remained inside—churning her belly and making her regret eating the cupcake.

"I'm afraid I have bad news. Just a moment. The police detective wishes to speak with you."

Isabella's grip tightened on her phone, and she strode through the cafe and into the kitchen. She was aware of Leo following, and that suited her. Solitary had been her MO, but now Leo was a fundamental part of her life. Important. She needed him.

"Mrs. Mitchell?" The masculine voice was low and gritty, a tad impatient.

"Yes," Isabella said.

"What is your relationship with Jaycee Howard?"

Isabella's mind worked, considering the angles. "We're long-time friends."

"I see. Did you know she put your name down as a contact?"

MY PRECIOUS GIFT

"I did," Isabella said, becoming angry at the prodding but restraining her temper because that wouldn't help. Impatience now, that was a different story. "Who are you? Why did the hospice contact me?"

"Detective Jones-White," he said, and she could hear the hesitation in his voice.

He didn't want to share until he checked her out. Her mind went through her mental list of contacts in Melbourne. Who could she trust to get her information on Jaycee without causing backlash for her current life in Middlemarch?

"Detective Jones-White, please tell me what has happened." Isabella spoke in a crisp, no-nonsense voice, one that showed her displeasure with his reticence.

The man issued a sigh, and instinct told her he used his cranky disposition as a front. Something about this situation—whatever it was—disturbed him.

"Ms. Mitchell, someone murdered your friend tonight."

Chapter 11

Bad News

Leo heard the detective and reached for Isabella. He slid her close and experienced the jolt that raced through her tense body.

"How?" Isabella asked in a faint voice.

"Fatally stabbed. The night attendee found her."

"Someone knifed a woman dying from cancer? Someone who'd gone to the hospice to die?" Isabella asked, her pain clear as she sought confirmation. Facts.

"Yes," Detective Jones-White said. "I'm sorry for your loss, and I promise I will do everything in my power to capture this scum."

"Thank you," Isabella said, resorting to politeness.

Leo frowned. She mightn't have seen Jaycee for years, but for Kian's sake, they needed to learn the truth about her death.

"May I speak with him?" Leo whispered to Isabella.

She started and turned her face to him. Astonishingly, her eyes were full of unshed tears. Astonishing because Isabella seldom let her emotions rule. She was the most self-contained and strong person he knew.

"Let me speak to the detective," he said, trying to communicate without words that he'd do his best to find answers for her and Kian. The tiny boy deserved to learn the truth once he grew older.

Isabella gave a curt nod and handed over the phone.

"Detective Jones-White. I'm Leo Mitchell, Isabella's husband. Isabella can't talk right now, but I know she'll have questions. What can you share with me?"

The detective hesitated before he spoke. "The night attendant saw a man in a black coat. She didn't see his face because he wore a black cap pulled low. He was tall and slender and knocked her to the floor when she asked what he was doing in Ms. Howard's room. The guy ran past her, and she thought he'd left."

"He didn't leave?"

"No, while the attendant was busy, the intruder searched the office. He took a copy of Ms. Howard's file, or at least someone left the file open on the computer, and the night attendant said it wasn't her. We caught him on camera while he was in the office. A receptionist recognized him and told me he'd visited earlier in the week. He told her he was Ms. Howard's husband."

"No," Leo said. "Jaycee's husband was Nepalese. He died in an avalanche about a year ago."

"You're certain of this?"

"Yes. Jaycee left her son with us, Detective. My wife is the boy's legal guardian. Jaycee left us her important records so we could share them with Kian when he was older. I've seen Jaycee's marriage certificate and her husband's death certificate. Apart from us, Jaycee's son has no close living relatives that we know of."

"Can you send me copies of the marriage and death certificates?" the detective asked. "I could search myself, but it'd take time my team could use to better advantage."

Leo glanced at Isabella, and she nodded approval.

"We'll do that, Detective. Is there an email we can send copies to?"

The detective rattled off his email address, and Leo jotted it down.

"Should we worry about security for Jaycee's son?" Leo asked.

"I don't know. I'll have more information once our inquiries proceed. Can I ring you again? I might have more questions."

"Detective, although my wife and Jaycee were close friends, their paths diverged. Isabella hadn't seen Jaycee for several years until recently."

"Yet she left her son with you. She trusted you to raise her child."

"At one time, they were close. Jaycee's son is a delight, and given the circumstances, we are happy to have him in our lives."

"Few people would consent to that big a favor," the detective said.

"I come from a large family. My brothers and I still live in the town where we grew up. There are plenty of children around for Jaycee's son to play with. He's better here than shoved into an institution."

"There is always a call for children from adoptive parents."

"Jaycee's last wish was that we bring up her son and keep him safe. That is what we intend to do." Leo didn't bother to keep the fierceness from his tone. "Please call if you have further information." Leo hung up and turned to Isabella.

"Thank you," she said.

Leo took her into his arms and hugged her hard, the urge for physical contact strong. He didn't have a good feeling about this situation.

"Something wrong?" Saber asked from the kitchen entrance.

Leo silently sought Isabella's permission, and she gave it with a nod. "Yes," he said. "Someone murdered Kian's mother at the hospice tonight. Someone stabbed her and fled after stealing her file."

"Didn't she have terminal cancer?" Saber asked.

"Yes, she didn't have long to live," Isabella said. "Leo, we'll have to tell Kian."

"Are you ready to leave?" Saber asked. "I'm taking our kids home since they're getting snappy."

"I'll get Kian," Isabella said.

"Stay," Saber said. "I'll round up the troops. They're running around outside in the garden." He retreated, leaving Leo alone with Isabella.

"This will be hard," Isabella said. "Telling Kian. I was wondering if we leave it until the morning when he isn't so tired. That way, we might have more information."

"Yes, that's a good idea," Leo said, a clamp tightening around his chest. He forced himself to inhale deeply, memories of their Uncle Herbert sitting them down to tell them about their parents' unexpected deaths swimming through his mind. He'd been seven. The news had taken a long time to register—the truth that his parents would never return from their Queenstown outing. The one shining beacon had been his Uncle Herbert and his brothers.

Adversity had brought the siblings closer. As children, they'd been fiercely protective of each other, and once they grew to adulthood and married, they'd remained close. While he had many other friends, his four brothers were his constant support. He grinned at a memory because after Uncle Herbert had passed away, Saber had taken charge. The oldest of the Mitchell clan, Saber, had put up with a lot of mischief until, one by one, they'd found their mates.

"What are you thinking?" Isabella asked.

"I was thinking about when my parents died. It was hard. Distressing. Confusing. You've heard about Uncle Herbert. Looking back, we didn't appreciate him as much as we should've. He was a bachelor, although he had oodles of charm and was never short of feminine company. I don't know why he never married. He was my father's older brother, and he took charge of us without hesitation. He moved into the house—the one where Saber and

Emily live now—and put his immediate life on hold."

"You don't talk about him much."

"We should. Our uncle was amazing and kept us together when it couldn't have been easy taking on five boys. After he died, we were older and full of mischief. I'm sure you've heard Saber complaining we're the reason his hair turned gray."

"He hasn't got gray hair," Isabella said, cocking her head, her expression one of confusion.

"No, but he said it so often, Felix suggested we turn it gray for him. The twins discovered spray-on color, and we sneaked into Saber's bedroom to do the dirty deed."

"What happened?"

"Saber heard us creeping around. He put pillows in his bed and this old doll with black hair. It was dark, and all we saw was the black hair. It smelled funny, of lavender. That should've been a warning sign, but we were excited to get one over big brother."

"Saber caught you."

"Yep, he waited until we'd committed the crime, then switched on the light. We got a hell of a fright. I might've squeaked," Leo confessed with a grin.

"What did Saber do after that?"

Leo pulled a face. "He had us on housework duty for the next two weeks, and none of us could visit our friends after school."

"Kian doesn't have brothers or sisters," Isabella said.

"He has cousins and aunts and uncles who will support him. I'm not saying it will be easy, but our family will help."

"Your family is special," Isabella said.

"It's easy to see that now, but we took Uncle Herbert and later Saber for granted."

Isabella reached for his hand and squeezed it. "I doubt either of them thought that. When is Saber's next birthday? Hold a surprise party for him and give him an engraved trophy that says that."

"Hmm," Leo said, pondering this. "That's a great idea. I'll give it more thought. Let's say our goodbyes and head home."

Once they reached home, Leo lifted a drowsy Kian out of his car seat and dropped him into Isabella's arms.

She took two steps and hesitated. "Maybe we should up our security until we discover if this attack was random or targeted."

Leo paused and swiveled to check her expression. "But no one except the family knows about Jaycee and how she left Kian on our doorstep."

"We know Kian's father is dead because we have a copy of the death certificate. They ruled his death accidental. But what about other relatives? Could there be someone in the background we're not aware of? Jaycee had money set aside for Kian. It's not a huge amount, but if someone was desperate..."

"It might be nothing," Leo said, but after Isabella planted the words, he wondered. "I'll do a circuit of the property as soon as you get Kian inside. I can't smell anything out of place. Can you?"

Isabella inhaled through her mouth, testing the distinct scents—the mowed grass, the sweet flower scent drifting from the pots of summer flowers, the duller dust and dirt of the sunbaked earth. "No, nothing that shouldn't be present."

"I'll go inside with you before I check outside," Leo stated.

Although Isabella could protect herself and Kian, Leo preferred to reassure himself. He grabbed the picnic basket and their rug, slammed their vehicle rear shut, and locked it. That done, he trotted up the footpath leading to the front entrance. He unlocked the door, silently congratulating himself on completing this task. He wasn't certain what had made him do this before they left, but he had gone against tradition. When they were kids, their parents had never locked doors or placed security locks on their windows.

Funny how responsibility for a child and changing times made one's thoughts alter.

While Isabella settled a sleepy Kian in bed, Leo prowled the house but found nothing out of place, nothing to ratchet up his fears even further. He returned to Isabella. "Nothing. I'll check outside now."

"Good idea that we decided to talk to Kian in the morning," she said. "He went to sleep as soon as his head hit the pillow."

"Poor little man. I feel so sorry for him." Leo did the rounds outside, but he discovered nothing to disturb him. Once inside again, he locked the front and rear doors and checked the windows. He shut every one of them, apart from their bedroom window.

Both he and Isabella would hear if intruders attempted to enter this way.

Isabella arrived in their bedroom a few minutes later. "It's a late night for Kian, and he didn't have a nap this afternoon. We still have to fix the Christmas tree. There are Kian signs everywhere—toys, clothes, pine tree needles—and that's just the lounge."

Leo grinned. "He has the makings of an excellent Mitchell already. That's the sort of mischief my brothers and I would've got up to at his age. All those shiny balls to play with."

An unexpected chortle escaped Isabella. "His expression was priceless. He didn't expect the tree to topple."

"We could put a ball in his Christmas stocking. Something big and durable."

"I was wondering if he might like prayer bells. You know, the Tibetan ones. Something to remind him of home."

"Where would you find those?" Leo asked.

"You can find practically anything on the net." Isabella pulled her silky tee over her head and tossed it in the laundry hamper. Her grin turned a trifle mocking as she turned back to him. "If not the normal web, then the dark one."

Leo shucked his clothes and grinned at his incredibly cute wife. "When you're searching the web, check for outdoor arts and crafts projects or things he could collect outside and bring indoors. Is he too young for a camera?"

"Yes, but we should take photos whenever we're out and about. Jaycee has made an online photographic book for him to have when he's older. We should do the same, starting with his life from now."

"Aw, look at us with the parenting," Leo murmured.

Isabella slid into bed, her expression turning somber. "Putting items in a Christmas stocking is the straightforward part. Telling Kian tomorrow his mother is dead—that will suck."

Chapter 12

Run Into Danger

Isabella woke with a start, every one of her senses on high alert. She didn't move a muscle, listening carefully for a repeat of the sound that had woken her. When that produced nothing, she opened her mouth and inhaled, keeping the movement unhurried and silent.

As her mind cataloged the distinct scents—the wildness of Leo's feline, his favorite cedar aftershave, and the whiff of lavender that drifted through the bedroom window—a less familiar one struck her. An instant later, a furry missile sprang onto the bed and jumped into the slight gap between her and Leo.

Isabella relaxed and tried not to smile at the snow leopard cub. "Hey, Kian," she whispered. A glance at her wristwatch told her it was almost five. It wouldn't be long before the birds started their dawn chorus. She grinned at Kian. "Did you wake early?"

Kian released a soft mew and pressed close to her hand.

Ah! He'd done this before, and she knew exactly what he wanted. She ran her hand over his silky back and stroked him. His blue eyes closed to mere slits, and a purr rumbled from him.

Leo rolled over to face them. "Kian."

"He woke up early and decided to say good morning."

"I see," Leo said. "Well, since we're all awake and it's still dark, why don't we go for a run?"

Kian immediately gave a mew of approval.

Isabella smiled, although her lips flattened an instant later. Today, they had to tell Kian about Jaycee. It was way too early to call the hospice or the detective since New Zealand was two hours ahead of Melbourne. "I think we should run. Kian is making gingerbread men this morning, so we can't take too long."

"He is?" Leo said. "Where?"

"Tomasine is taking charge of the kids this morning. I believe London and Caroline will be there along with their kids."

"A recipe for chaos," Leo said.

"I wouldn't shudder too much. Emily has organized a roster. You and I are in charge of a sports day for the kids."

"Why am I just learning this?" Leo croaked, aghast.

"It happens every year, but we've never had a turn because we didn't have children. Now we have Kian, so Emily shunted us into the roster."

"Oh." Leo switched on the bedside light and stared at Isabella for an extended moment. His breath hissed out as realization struck him. "You felt left out."

Isabella gave an irritable shrug. "Emily and Tomasine always included me, but I always volunteered to mind the café. I tried not to feel sorry for myself. Failed."

"Aw, Isabella. Why didn't you say something?"

"Because we couldn't fix the problem, and it was my fault." Isabella glanced away, appalled to find herself close to tears.

"We'll talk about this later," Leo stated, and he sounded miffed.

Isabella's shoulders slumped. "Okay."

Leo's scowl softened. "Isabella, it'll be all right. I promise."

She nodded, guilt doing a number on her because she hadn't been fair to Leo. She understood this but had kept her pain inside, anyway. And it wasn't as if today wouldn't be challenging enough. She bounded out of bed and shifted to a snow leopard.

Kian's expression and his wide blue eyes made her want to laugh. They hadn't explained to him she could shift into any form she wanted.

On impulse, she shifted into Leo's form.

"Oh no," Leo protested, holding his hands in front of him. "Not that again. I couldn't kiss you for days after seeing my face looking back at me."

"I'll open the door," Isabella said, but she sounded exactly like Leo. "Come along, Kian."

Kian cocked his kitty head, obviously confused.

"Go with Isabella," Leo said when the boy didn't move. "We'll run in the dark and return before anyone can see us."

Kian jumped off the bed and trotted from the room. Leo followed, remained in his human form until he closed the door. Typically, they'd leave the entrance unsecured, but Isabella silently approved when he locked it and placed the key under a rock near the mailbox. Once he shifted, the trio trotted down the driveway and into the first paddock on the left.

Isabella had taken the form of a snow leopard again, and she noticed Kian seemed taken by this. Of course! All the Mitchells were black leopard shifters, and she'd always assumed that form, so she didn't stand out. But now that they had Kian in their lives, she could take either form. If she helped Kian feel at home by doing this small thing, that's what she'd do.

They stayed out for an hour, running and jumping and playing tag.

Daylight had arrived, and the distant hum of a tractor floated to them along with early morning commuter traffic driving to Dunedin or one of the closer towns. Their house sat in a private lane, but they needed caution since several other families lived on the same road.

Leo took the lead, setting a brisk pace. Isabella shunted Kian forward with her nose and urged him to trot after Leo. She loped in the rear.

The drone of an approaching vehicle had Leo tensing. Isabella growled and urged Kian into the undergrowth on the side of the road. Kian's coloring and her snow leopard pelt blended with the dry, straw-like undergrowth. Leo's black fur didn't camouflage as well.

Isabella let out a demanding yowl, and Leo read her mind. He darted into the undergrowth and pressed close to the hedge that edged the paddock. Isabella took the spot nearest the road, and they squeezed Kian between them. Isabella put her head down, her body tense as the vehicle approached. It wasn't a local. She could tell because each car had a distinct sound.

Perhaps a visitor? It was early for strangers to drive up their road. She lifted her head, keeping the movement slow to avoid detection. The car drove at a leisurely pace, making it simple to glimpse the driver. He wore dark glasses and his hair was black with hints of silver. That was all she noted before the car passed. One last thing sank into her brain. The vehicle was a rental since it had a sticker on the back window.

Once the driver rounded a bend in the road, Isabella sprang up and released an urgent bark—an order to act immediately. Kian scurried after her with Leo at the rear. They'd reached their driveway when they heard the car return. The three of them darted behind a leafy bush covered with purple flowers.

The car crawled past, taking long moments before the engine whirr retreated. Leo shifted and grabbed the key. He ran to the front door, unlocked and opened it before Isabella shunted Kian from hiding, and they raced into the house.

Leo shut and locked the door behind them. "I'll give Kian a quick shower before we have breakfast and a talk?"

Everything inside Isabella clenched with fear. Sorrow. Compassion and anxiety. But she managed a nod and pushed out a few words. "Thanks, Leo. That would be great. I'll take a shower before I start breakfast. It feels like a pancake morning."

Leo was somber as he nodded and guided Kian, still in his kitten form, toward the bathroom. The old pipes groaned when Leo turned the taps, and this familiar sound pushed her to hustle. She grabbed clean underwear and took a brisk, tepid shower. Once she'd pulled a brush through her hair and dressed in shorts and a T-shirt, she hurried to the kitchen.

By the time Leo arrived with Kian, she had the coffee underway and the pancake batter mixed. Breakfast was a somber affair. Kian appeared to enjoy his pancakes but, as usual, didn't chatter. Isabella would've worried about his silence, but he was interacting and talking with the other children, so she figured he still needed time to become used to her and Leo, their routine.

Isabella kept a close eye on him while pretending to eat. The pancake resembled sawdust, and the thick pieces clogged her throat. No amount of coffee cleared the spongy obstruction. Leo didn't do any better with his breakfast and gave up, shoving his uneaten pancakes away.

MY PRECIOUS GIFT

They had to inform Kian about Jaycee's death.

"Kian." Isabella wet her lips and curled her trembling hands into balls. This was hard. No matter how much she wanted to run and hide to avoid hurting this shifter boy, she couldn't. She was the adult here, and Jaycee's dying wish had been for Isabella to become Kian's guardian. The boy was sweet and mischievous and quiet because he was still finding his way, but she'd fallen in love with him. Isabella needed Kian as much as he needed her and Leo. Kian was her chance for a family. She admitted and reveled in this fact. Crap. what sort of person did that make her? Jaycee had sacrificed everything to keep her son safe, and Isabella could do nothing less than her absolute best.

"Kian," she said again. "We need to tell you something."

The boy cocked his head, a lock of his hair swinging against his cheek. His blue gaze bored into her as he fixed his attention. Isabella swallowed hard, but it was a wasted effort.

Beneath the table, Leo reached for her hand. His solid presence gave her a shot of backbone.

"The people at the hospice where your mama went called me last night," she said, watching his wee face closely.

"Mama?" he whispered, studying her intently now.

"Yes. Kian, your mama died last night."

The boy nodded, his eyes huge in his tiny face. "Mama," he said, his voice whisper-soft. "She is an angel now?"

Tears pricked Isabella's eyes, and one rolled down her cheek without permission. Leo's hand tightened on hers, and when she glanced at him, she spotted his approval and encouragement.

"Yes, your mama makes a pretty angel."

Another tear escaped, but Isabella didn't brush it away. Jaycee had done a masterful job with her son, planning everything to make her passing as easy as possible. She'd prepared Kian for this day and talked to him about her death. Relief warred with regret that she'd lost touch with her friend. Right then, Isabella made herself a promise to help keep Jaycee alive in Kian's memories. When he was older, they'd take a trip to Nepal and visit Kian's birth country. Something else occurred to her, and she edged closer to Kian.

"Would..." She hesitated and cleared her throat yet again, unsure if her idea was dumb or if she should run it past Leo first. Leo was a people person and had better instincts than her. She glanced at her husband, and it was his steady and encouraging smile that bolstered her courage. "Kian, we could have a special angel party for your mama. So she knows we're happy for her and glad she is watching over us."

When neither Kian nor Leo uttered a word, doubt plagued Isabella again. She glanced at Leo. "Is this a bad idea?"

"It's a brilliant plan, sweetheart." Leo's whisper was for her ears only.

But did Kian think the same? He was four. Trepidation churned her stomach as she forced herself to study Kian. Lordy, she was an adult, an ex-assassin who feared nothing, yet this child left her shaking in her shoes. Jaycee had been wrong about Isabella's abilities. Child-rearing wasn't in her talent bucket.

"When?" Kian's lyrical voice cut through her panic, and her mouth dropped open.

"Sweetheart," Leo said, sounding amused. He used his free hand to tap a finger on her gaping lips. "When will we have the angel party?"

"Um." Isabella frantically thought about the days ahead. Not many days now until Christmas. "What about at the family get-together on Christmas Eve?"

"Perfect," Leo said. "In twelve sleeps," he told Kian. "We'll have a party for your mama. It will be a busy week because the next day is Christmas. Santa will visit. If you behave, he'll leave presents in your Christmas stocking." Leo paused. "Isabella, do we have a stocking?"

"On my list. Tomasine and I are going shopping tomorrow to get …ah…things," she added, recalling small ears were in the vicinity and listening.

Leo nodded, taking her meaning. "Kian, we'll be ready for Santa's visit."

Kian's small face scrunched up. "How does Mr. Saber deliver presents to everyone? He works on the farm."

Leo guffawed, and Isabella found her lips twitching. How to explain?

"Santa is a busy man," Leo said, recovering first. "Saber was helping him out and agreed to wear a disguise. Saber wore the red suit so Santa could have a rest ahead of the biggest day of his year."

"Oh," Kian said.

Isabella couldn't tell if Kian believed Leo because the child possessed a poker face, but Leo deserved a big kiss for coming up with that explanation.

Chapter 13

Gingerbread Men

Kian ate the rest of his pancakes with relish, the only one of them who'd done justice to their breakfast. Isabella poured more coffee and tried to smother the prickling danger signals within her.

"What does Kian need to take to Tomasine's?" Leo asked. "Do we need to pack him a bag?"

"His swimming trunks and a towel. Felix intends to take the kids swimming while the gingerbread men are cooking."

"Right. I'll pack those." Leo paused and glanced at Kian, his mouth pulled into a frown.

Leo's thoughts traveled the same path as hers. Kian was dealing with his mother's death well. Was this the correct reaction? Hell, if she knew. She hadn't cried or wailed when her parents passed. She'd carried on, the absence of her parents a mere blip in her routine.

The difference between her and Kian's situations was vast, however, because Jaycee had loved Kian. That was easy to tell in the care she'd taken to leave Kian a life record and the research she'd done to locate Isabella. Their meeting at the café had been an interview for parenthood—one Isabella must've passed.

There was one glaring omission. In all the documents, Isabella had noticed nothing relating to Jaycee's family. She'd mentioned them in the café—told Isabella she intended to meet her family in Greece. Why? This hadn't struck her earlier because she'd been in panic mode. Why had Jaycee ignored her family when they were the obvious choice to take custody of their grandson? Had they not approved of Kian's father?

She had a lot to research in the coming week. Also, the rental car that had passed them early this morning. That had been strange. The driver might've taken the wrong turning on Middlemarch's confusing country roads, or perhaps they had family in the area—another thing to check. She'd watch for the brown rental car in case it popped up in her vicinity again.

Isabella saw Kian had finished and cleared the last of the breakfast dishes.

"Have you made a gingerbread man before?" she asked.

His brow puckered, and he shook his head. Isabella waited for him to speak, but his blue gaze remained trained on her, and he stayed silent. He had a healthy portion of pancake syrup smeared across his mouth.

"Have you read the story of the gingerbread man?"

His eyes brightened. "Yes."

Encouraged, Isabella sought something else to say. Ah! Brainwave. "I'm sure Tomasine will have the book. Should we ask to borrow it, and we can read it to you tonight?"

"Yes, please." He beamed this time, and Isabella was quite certain she was smiling back because *small wins*.

Leo reappeared. "The office rang. There's a problem with the labeling machine. I'm off to fix it. Should I drive you to the café?"

"Can you drop us at Tomasine's place? I'll walk from there."

"Sure thing." Leo handed the backpack over to her and glanced at Kian. "We'd better do face washing and teeth cleaning before we leave."

Obediently, Kian climbed off his chair and ambled away with Leo.

Isabella hustled to the bedroom to grab her handbag. She stepped over a toy truck and a bulldozer, scooping them up. She had already dressed in the café uniform T-shirt and wore long shorts in deference to the heat.

When they arrived at Tomasine and Felix's house, Saber was dropping off his girls. He climbed out of the car, unbuckled his daughters' car seats, and handed them a bag each before kissing them goodbye.

"We need to do that," Isabella murmured to Leo. "It's a parent thing, although mine never farewelled me."

"Your parents were idiots," Leo stated in a brook-no-refusal tone as they watched the girls run into the house. "Hey, Saber. Do you need help later this week?"

"That'd be fantastic. I could do with mustering volunteers."

"Me?" Kian asked, pushing past Isabella, who'd unbuckled his car seat. He appeared tiny compared to the two men but showed no nervousness. This idea excited him.

Saber crouched in front of Kian. "Would you help us muster the sheep?"

"Yes." Enthusiasm shone in the boy.

"As long as Leo and Isabella say yes, then it's okay with me," Saber said. "You were a big help last time."

"Which day?" Leo asked.

"The weather forecast looks good for the next two weeks at least," Saber said. "I thought we'd start early on Thursday morning before it gets too hot."

"All right. Kian and I will be there to help. Right, Kian?"

"Yes!" Kian beamed and threw himself at Saber. His skinny arms wrapped around Saber's neck, and he hugged Leo's surprised brother before bounding toward Leo. Leo ducked to Kian's height and received the same hearty hug.

The flash of emotion on Leo's face brought relief, followed by a twinge of jealousy. Isabella quashed that errant sensation immediately. "How late will you be?"

"It depends on how difficult the label machine is," Leo said with a grin. "I'll call you. You're working at the café all day?"

"Yes. Tomasine won't mind keeping Kian for the afternoon, or he can spend it in the café."

Leo nodded and gave Isabella a quick kiss that left her breathless.

Leo and Saber drove off together.

"What did you do with your mama?" She should've asked that earlier.

"Color pictures and play games."

Inside activities. For an active shifter child, that must've been hard. Although Jaycee had provided lots of information, Isabella was clueless about the minor things. She needed to learn from Emily and Tomasine what she should teach him. She sighed, once again feeling as if her feet weren't touching the ground. Give her a gun or a knife—any type of weapon—and it was an extension to her hand. She had complete control and understood the steps to receive the outcome she wanted. Assassin 101. This parenting stuff was heaps harder, and she feared making a catastrophic mess and marking Kian for life.

She greeted Tomasine with a broad smile. Kian tugged her hand, and in surprise, she glanced down at him.

"Gingerbread man," he said.

"Oh. Right. Tomasine, do you have the gingerbread man story?"

"Yes, of course. How about if Kian helps me to pack books and one or two games for you to borrow? The boys are full of enthusiasm for books and games, but they grow sick of them, and they get consigned to the cupboard." She paused, a strange expression on her face. "You know, I bet lots of other families have the same situation. Our boys own lots of toys and books because we spoil them. In the New Year, we should set up a library of toys and kid's books for any resident to borrow."

Isabella nodded, seeing the sense of that. "It's a wonderful idea. London would be the best person to contact since she's on the Feline Council. If you get their approval, it will be much easier."

Isabella squatted in front of Kian. "You be good for Tomasine, okay?"

He nodded.

Isabella wanted to hug him. She hesitated, then went for it. She placed her hands on his shoulders and embraced him, breathing in his little boy smell and the hint of soap and laundry powder that came with him. Her heart battered her ribs when he hugged her back briefly.

When he stopped, she took this as the cue to release him and stood.

"Thanks, Tomasine."

"Any time. You babysat for me so often—I owe you big time."

Isabella watched Kian run off with Saber's girls. She waited until he'd rounded a corner, but she still lowered her voice. "We told Kian his mother had died this morning. Not the full truth—that someone murdered her—but he knows she died."

Tomasine frowned. "He seemed normal."

"Yeah. Jaycee had prepared him and told him she'd turn into an angel who watched over him. Tomasine, she was an amazing parent. She's left photos and records for Kian when he grows older." Her throat knotted up in what was becoming a regular occurrence. She swallowed hard and pushed her next words past the partial blockage. "Should Leo and I worry about his calm acceptance?"

"Oh, Isabella." Tomasine squeezed Isabella's upper arm. "You're doing everything right. You've talked to him, and you're keeping him busy. Felix told me Kian kept up with him and Saber easily, and Kian has brilliant tracking skills. He's quiet but interacts with the other kids, and at this time of the year, there is plenty to do. We'll watch over him too. You'll get there. Just try to keep him talking. Talk about Jaycee and keep her real for her son."

"I've printed a photo of Jaycee and her husband and framed it for Kian to keep by his bed. He seems to treasure that."

"Perfect. You could let Kian choose his favorite photos to put in one of those small brag books. That way, he could flick through the photos anytime."

"We told him we'll have an angel party on Christmas Eve for Jaycee, and he seemed quite taken with that. Can we do that?" Isabella shrugged. "Maybe wear white and have a special cake?"

Tomasine stood on tiptoe and hugged Isabella. "I can tell you're panicking about this parenting gig, but you and Leo are rockin' it. I'll talk to Emily, and there's no reason we couldn't make this a Christmas Eve tradition."

"Thank you."

Tomasine flapped her hand in dismissal. "Unnecessary."

Isabella turned to leave before halting. "One more thing. We ran early this morning and had to dive for cover when a vehicle drove past our house. The driver turned around and returned moments later, so they might've taken the wrong turn. Watch for a brown rental car when you're out and about today."

Tomasine's gaze narrowed. "I will," she promised. "I'll let Felix and Sylvie know too."

"Thanks. Drop Kian at the café when you're ready for a rest."

Isabella usually enjoyed the walk to the café, but today, her nerves jangled, her instincts screaming of impending danger. The brown rental car, or was it Jaycee's murder that had her anxiety blooming like a summer flower?

After checking the time, she contacted the policeman she'd spoken to the previous evening. "It's Isabella Mitchell," she said when the detective answered the phone. "I wondered if you have any other information about my friend? Do you have a motive? It can't be a robbery—not in a hospice. Someone targeted Jaycee because, otherwise, none of this makes sense."

The detective gave a rusty chuckle. "Can I have a turn to talk?"

"Sorry," Isabella muttered, heat rising in her cheeks. At the finish of Tomasine and Felix's driveway, she turned right. A bird sang from the depths of a roadside hedge while she waited for the detective to speak.

His sigh echoed down the line. "You're right. Nothing about this crime makes sense. Jaycee was dying. The medical staff told me she didn't have long. The day nurse who monitored Jaycee said she wasn't bedridden but was deteriorating rapidly. She hasn't noted any missing items. Jaycee had few possessions. Her tablet was under her pillow, but no phone anywhere."

"You're being remarkably forthcoming." Isabella lifted her face to the warmth of the sun, needing the heat since the detective's words had sent an icy shiver through her.

"Because this murder sickens me, and I don't have a single clue to further our investigation. The hospice didn't have security cameras, apart from in the pharmacy where they keep drugs. Nothing obvious has gone, nor does it appear anyone attempted to enter the locked room. Do you know anything about Jaycee's family?"

"All I know is they live in Greece. Santorini. Jaycee told me she intended to visit them for Christmas." Isabella hesitated because the detective hadn't mentioned Kian. "Jaycee's husband was Nepalese and died in an avalanche in Nepal. Leo told you Jaycee left her young son with us. I'm his legal guardian."

"Why didn't she leave her son with her family?" The detective's voice emerged sharp and alert.

"I don't know." Although she had an inkling of an idea, and it was shifter-related. "I don't even know if Jaycee's family are aware she has a son."

"Oh?"

Isabella weighed her words before she spoke. "Jaycee left me photos and other family memorabilia to give her son when he is older. The photos are of her husband's family rather than Jaycee's. I've found photos of English relatives—I'm unsure of the connection yet—but none from Greece."

"You think there was an argument or a family dispute?"

"Possibly. If you decide to approach the family, I think it would be best not to mention Jaycee's son."

"The paperwork giving you guardianship is legal?"

"It is." Or it would be once she and Leo signed the document and presented it to their lawyer. Isabella made a mental note to ring for an appointment and organize the paperwork this evening. Jaycee needed them to follow through now more than ever.

"Thank you for this information. Jaycee only listed you as a contact at the hospice." The man hesitated. "Whoever stabbed her did a good job of it. There was no hesitation. I'd go as far to say the culprit hated Jaycee with a passion."

"No one heard anything?" Isabella asked.

"The occupants of the nearby rooms are near the end and heavily medicated."

"Can I ring you again?"

"Yes, and if you learn anything else, please contact me immediately. This murder doesn't sit well with me." His sigh was harsh. "Some crime scenes are worse than others."

"Thank you for sharing information," Isabella said. "Do you know if Jaycee's funeral is proceeding soon?"

"You'll need to speak to the hospice management."

"Thanks, I will," Isabella said.

Isabella disconnected and checked the time. Although it might make her late to work, she detoured to the police station to speak with Laura and Charlie. In the past, she'd worked with them on cases, given her specific skill set.

She noted the two parked police cars when she turned the corner. She jogged up the stairs and came face-to-face with Suzie and Edwina. The teens snarled at her and stomped outside.

"Something I said?" she quipped to Charlie.

"I'll deny this should you ever repeat me, but those two girls are trouble waiting to happen. This time, their behavior horrified their grandmothers, and they didn't pull rank to get their granddaughters out of their punishment. What brings you here today?"

"We might have a problem. Can I speak in private? I need to make it fast since Emily is expecting me at the café."

"Sure." Curiosity blazed in Charlie's expression. "Should I grab Laura too?"

"It would save time," Isabella said.

"We'll go to Laura's office," Charlie said.

Five minutes later, Isabella was busy telling Laura and Charlie her tale about Jaycee's visit, Kian arriving on their doorstep, and then the call from the police in Melbourne.

"Someone murdered a dying woman?" Laura asked.

"Yeah, from what the detective told me, it was a frenzied attack. But that's not all. This morning a brown rental car drove past our house. After a few minutes, it returned and continued to the main road. Normally, we wouldn't have noticed, but Kian woke us early, and the three of us went for a run."

Although Laura and Charlie were humans, they had feline mates and kept the feline community's secrets close to their chest.

"You're wondering if your friend's murder might have something to do with her son," Laura said. "Her family, perhaps? Especially since Jaycee left her son with you rather than her relations. You said that the boy's father is dead?"

"Yes, and his grandparents," Isabella said. "This brown car, its appearance might be innocent, but my gut is saying otherwise. It was early—too early for tourists or visitors to the area. People driving at that time of the morning know where they're going. They don't get lost."

Chapter 14

High Alert

The café was busier than usual, with a busload of older women from Dunedin. Isabella kept busy delivering plates of sandwiches, cheese scones, and strawberry tarts, along with pots of tea. Once the women strolled back to their bus, she scrambled to clear tables and stack the dishwasher.

She didn't have time to chat with locals or scrutinize strangers since so many hovered in the vicinity. Isabella finally managed a break around two, and she sat at a garden table with a ham sandwich, a strawberry tart, and a chocolate milkshake. She'd taken one bite of sandwich when Tomasine arrived with Kian and her two boys.

"Emily said you've been busy," Tomasine said. "You should've rung me. Either Sylvie or I could've pitched in to help."

Isabella snorted. "Too harried to ring. It was crazy busy. Saber and Felix helped for about half an hour before they had to leave. We knew the sizeable group was coming, and we had plenty of food, but we weren't aware the number had grown, and they'd hired a bigger bus."

"Are you sure you want me to leave Kian here?" Tomasine asked.

"Here," Kian stated.

Tomasine shared a teasing glance with Isabella. "That's settled then."

Isabella ruffled Kian's hair and handed over a triangle of her sandwich. "We'll be fine. I promised Emily I'd work until five. Two part-timers are starting then. Ramsay is taking care of the early dinners, and we're shutting at eight."

"In that case, I'll go home and put up my feet. Maybe read a book in a shady spot on the verandah."

"Thanks for looking after Kian."

"Anytime."

"Hey, where's my gingerbread man? Did you make one for me?"

"The kids consumed the gingerbread men with a glass of milk. Not a crumb left." Tomasine laughed, then waved and headed off with her boys.

"What do you want to do?" she asked Kian. "You'll have to stay here until I finish work."

"Draw," Kian said.

"That we can do." She leaned closer. "Can you stay in two legs and not move from this table? Would you like a strawberry tart?"

"Yes. Please," he added.

"All right." She pushed the plate with her tart toward Kian. "I'll be inside helping Emily. If you need me, come and find me. Okay? You wait there while I get your paper and crayons. When you tire of drawing, you can come to the kitchen. I think Emily is baking cookies this afternoon."

He nodded, and Isabella hopped up to retrieve the drawing materials from the kid's corner.

"Remember, don't leave the café. You can stay in the garden or come to the kitchen. If you need anything, ask Emily or me. You remember Emily?"

"Yes." Kian's blue eyes were calm, his expression smooth and guileless.

Still, Isabella hesitated, which was stupid because Emily's and Tomasine's children regularly played in the café garden while their mothers worked. The children couldn't leave without walking through the main café. No, Jaycee's murder had placed her on edge. The car this morning might've been what it purported to be—a visitor to the area who'd become lost.

She forced a smile. "Why don't you draw a special picture for Leo, and we'll attach it to the fridge before he gets home?"

The suggestion brought a bright smile to Kian's face, and Isabella grinned in return. He was a great kid, and Jaycee had been a massive part of his character development. A wash of sadness tightened Isabella's chest, and she fervently wished she could rewind time and tell Jaycee how awesome her son was.

Aware of the passing time, Isabella cleared the dirty crockery from the empty tables and carried trays into the kitchen. She set straight to work, removing the debris off the plates and stacking them in the dishwasher.

"Isabella." Emily entered the kitchen. "Things are slackening off here. My two part-timers have things under control, so I'll start baking."

"Kian is drawing out in the garden," Isabella said. "I'm all yours, but I need to watch him."

"He'll be fine," Emily said. "But I'll mention him to the girls working the front. He's so well-behaved. How about if Saber and I swap you two girls for Kian?"

Isabella pulled a face since Emily's twins were a mischievous pair. "Leo and I are happy with Kian."

Emily chortled. "You should've seen your face!"

"Not funny."

Isabella helped to take orders, ran back and forth with dirty dishes, and acted as a sous chef for Emily. In between, she checked on Kian and gave him a cold drink. She took five minutes to sit with him.

"Was your gingerbread man tasty?"

"Drew a picture," Kian said and handed her a piece of paper.

He'd drawn a remarkably detailed and lifelike gingerbread man rather than the vague scribbles she'd expected.

"You're an artist," she said.

He beamed at her, the smile fading without warning. His head jerked up, and he stared at the hedge that edged the café garden and kept the area private from the sidewalk. His hair bristled, his feline pushing close to the surface. Isabella whirled to stare in the same direction, her pulse racing. Someone lingered there, but the hedge's density made it difficult to see a face.

"Wait there," she said to Kian. "Don't move."

Before she'd finished speaking, she'd glided into the café and darted out the front door. She glanced left and right, but all she spotted was a woman walking a dog. She considered roaming the block but didn't like to leave Kian's side. Isabella reentered the cafe and strode straight to Kian.

She slid onto the bench seat beside him.

"Do you know who that was?"

He shook his head.

"All right. You can do more drawing later. Come inside and work in the kitchen with Emily."

Kian nodded agreeably, and Isabella helped him to pack up the drawing materials. She studied the hedge and cast out her senses, but she couldn't see or hear anyone lurking nearby. The desire to hunt down the person responsible for scaring Kian ate at her, but she shoved it away and focused. Protecting Kian was more important right now.

· ♥ · ♥ · ♥ · ♥ · ♥ ·

Leo arrived home from his day at the vineyard, the scent of a meaty tomato sauce greeting him. He spotted Kian and Isabella through the kitchen window. Kian appeared to be helping Isabella to make a salad. Isabella mightn't think it, but she was a natural in the parenting stakes. She was firm yet allowed Kian to explore the world and try things himself. A messy child or dirty clothes didn't bother her in the slightest.

"Hey, I'm home," he called, surprised to find himself locked out of the house.

Alarm flashed through him as he waited for Isabella to open the door. The locks clicked, and the door swung ajar to reveal Isabella.

"Is something wrong?" he asked.

"Someone was spying on Kian while he was in the café garden. I couldn't see anyone, but Kian broke off what he was doing and stared. His hair bristled."

"Have you asked him about it?"

"I tried, but he couldn't tell me anything. He's going with you and Saber tomorrow to help muster. Maybe he'll talk then when he's more relaxed."

Leo reached for Isabella and folded her into his embrace. She leaned against him for an instant before she pushed away.

"I need to check on my pasta sauce."

"Hey, buddy," Leo said, smiling at Kian. Leo's heartbeat stuttered when Kian returned his smile and continued with the task Isabella had set him. Warmth spread through Leo—a fierce need to protect the young shifter. "That smells delicious. Do I have time for a shower?"

"Yes," Isabella said. "I don't suppose you saw the brown vehicle when you drove through the township?"

"No," Leo lowered his voice. "Has Kian spoken of Jaycee?"

"No. I don't understand it. Kian seems so calm."

"He's self-contained and has suffered a lot of loss during his brief life. All we can do is to be there should he need us."

"It doesn't seem enough." Doubt tinged Isabella's reply, and Leo understood the emotions that poured through his mate—the urgent need to safeguard. His wife, at heart, was a protector. It was her calling, and she was fiercely caring of those she loved.

An inner sense had Leo jolting. Both Isabella and Kian reacted, too, all three whirling to face the kitchen window.

Leo glimpsed a pale face before the man jerked from sight. Leo sprinted for the front door and tore outside without considering weapons or anything else. Before he reached the gate, a vehicle accelerated, tires screaming for purchase on the gravel. When Leo reached the end of the driveway and gained visibility of the road, he spotted a brown car streaking away.

Leo lifted his head, drawing a huge draft of air into his lungs. The lingering traces of a patchouli aftershave and a hint of sweat, but as far as he could tell, the man had been alone.

But what did he want? That was the question that plagued Leo.

Whatever was afoot, it was time to brief his brothers and fashion a plan. Leo returned to the house, locked the door, and entered the kitchen.

"Anything?" Isabella asked.

"Brown car," Leo said. "One person, as far as I could ascertain."

"My spidey senses are crawlin'," Isabella said. "I need to research, talk to the detective in Melbourne again."

Leo walked over to where Kian sat at the kitchen table. He crouched beside the boy. "Do you know the man? The one who looked through the window?"

"Bad man," Kian said. "Mama hate him."

Leo shared a glance with Isabella. "Do you know his name?"

Kian shook his head. "Bad man," he repeated.

"Why is he bad?" Leo kept his questions simple.

"He picked me up and ran away." Kian scowled, his forehead scrunched up as if terrible memories grasped him.

"He took you?" Isabella asked.

Kian nodded. "Mama got me back."

Despite questioning Kian, they gained no further information. In the end, they made a tactic agreement to cease their interrogation.

"I'll take that shower. After dinner, I'll call Saber," Leo said.

Isabella stirred her sauce and knocked the spoon against the top of the pot. "Ten minutes. Kian and I will set the table."

Leo helped Kian wash his hands and watched the boy, but he showed no aggravation or sadness. He concentrated fiercely on his task. "Did the letter that Jaycee mentioned turn up yet?"

"There was no mail today."

"Did she have your address?"

"Yes, I gave her a business card when we were at the café, so she had my phone number too."

"If you're speaking to the detective again, ask if there is an envelope there for you. Perhaps she didn't get time to post it."

"First, I want to research Jaycee's family. I've never met them, and she never discussed them. I'm not even sure how many siblings she has because I didn't encourage family talk. Not when mine was a hot mess." Isabella handed Leo a small bowl of penne pasta and the sauce topping. "That one is for Kian. I'll grab the garlic bread from the oven."

Leo set Kian's dinner on the table and helped him sit before accepting two more plates of food from Isabella. They were all seated a few minutes later, a garlic butter and pasta sauce richness filling the air.

"Dinner smells wonderful," Leo said. "Do you eat pasta, Kian?"

"Yes," Kian said with such enthusiasm Leo and Isabella laughed.

"I'm glad we have a night at home," Isabella said. "We can turn on the Christmas lights and enjoy them."

Kian's head came up at this, interest in his blue eyes.

"Did you know our lights play music?" Isabella asked.

Leo groaned. "I hate that music."

Isabella grinned in return, wrinkling her nose. "I know."

After dinner, the three of them watched a cartoon while the Christmas tree lights sparkled in the lounge's corner. Since they were watching TV, Leo persuaded Isabella not to switch on the lights' music until it was almost Kian's bedtime. He clapped his hands, and his eyes sparkled even as he yawned hugely.

MY PRECIOUS GIFT

Isabella carted him off to bed, and Leo called Saber to the distant sound of Isabella reading a bedtime story.

"Leo," Saber said. "Problem?"

"Yeah, we caught a guy peeking through our window earlier. He drove a brown rental—the same one we saw earlier this morning. He got away before we could nab him."

"You didn't recognize him?" Saber asked, his tone sharp.

"No, I've never seen him before. We talked to Kian. He called him a bad man. When we questioned him, he said the man had stolen him, and Jaycee had got him back. We didn't like to push harder for answers."

"Did whoever murdered Jaycee have time to get to New Zealand?"

"It'd be tight but doable," Leo said, having already considered this. "If someone—this guy—has already snatched Kian once, we need to take extra care."

"You're thinking this guy tracked Jaycee to Melbourne, confronted her, murdered her, then skedaddled to Dunedin."

"That's about the size of it," Leo agreed. "I'm leaning toward them wanting Kian as a lever to grab the money Jaycee left."

"Or worse, perhaps this person knows of Kian's shifter status and has other nefarious purposes," Saber said.

"That makes sense. If our working theory is correct, what do we do to stop this guy? And if he's after Kian because he's a shifter, what about the other kids? If that's the case, it mightn't matter to this guy which kid he grabs."

Chapter 15

Swimming and Ice Cream

"I hope that's not true," Isabella whispered, emerging from Kian's bedroom in time to hear Leo's comment. "We need a plan."

Saber must've heard because he said, "Contact your police detective in Melbourne and ask if he has further information about Jaycee's situation. Isabella can research the family while we gather our kids together with decent protection. The rest of us will hunt for this brown car, check the accommodation in the area. I'll speak to the Feline Council and give them a heads-up about the kids. Even if we're wrong, and it's Kian this person wants, overprotection won't hurt anyone."

"And if we don't find this brown rental car?" Leo asked.

"We patrol the town. Pull in everyone who can help. Watch and wait," Saber replied.

Isabella nodded approval. "We need to start tonight."

"Let's take Kian and my girls to Felix. Emily can go with them. Tomasine and Felix will be present and Sylvie is a sensible kid," Saber said. "The children should be safe enough with the four of them. I suggest we start a nightly patrol. We'll liaise with Laura and Charlie and ask for other volunteers."

"Sounds good," Leo said. "I'll drop Kian with you now and give Isabella a chance to start her research."

Isabella's starting point was the cloud info Jaycee had left her. She'd studied the photos and printed several for Kian. She'd already skimmed Kian's birth record, Jaycee's marriage certificate, and Kian's father's death certificate. But now, she dived deeper. She reviewed each photo with unidentified people before realizing not one contained anyone from Jaycee's natural family. Isabella thought over the times they'd worked together, and while Jaycee had spoken of her family, it'd been surface stuff. Nothing deep. Isabella hadn't noticed because she kept her info close to the chest too. Her parents had

MY PRECIOUS GIFT

been con-artists and grifters, and nothing in their behavior was boast-worthy.

Isabella pulled up the family tree Jaycee had included. She started and stared hard at one word that leaped off the page at her. *Adopted.* Jaycee's adopted parents were English with military backgrounds. But she'd started checking on her true family, and they were Greek and lived on Santorini.

Jaycee had mentioned them, but was it only recently? To her shame, Isabella couldn't remember. She should've been a better friend, but in her defense, she'd struggled with the family concept since hers had been so awful. It wasn't until she'd met Tomasine that she comprehended the bonds of love. Mating with Leo had provided a concrete example of how a decent family functioned. Each of the Mitchells had wrapped Isabella into their close-knit group and claimed her loyalty.

Now, with the names of Jaycee's birth parents, Isabella deepened her research. Half an hour later, a picture emerged, and not a pretty one. Jaycee's parents lived on Santorini and hadn't married. Jaycee had dodged a horrid childhood, given the two irresponsible and spoiled twenty-somethings who'd created her.

Had Jaycee contacted them? Met them?

Surely, she would've done her research first if she had? But, if she'd gone searching not long after her husband's death, when she'd been vulnerable with a baby to care for, she might've forgone deep investigation and acted on instinct.

Leo arrived back at the house with Saber on his heels.

"Any luck with the research?" Leo asked.

"An English military couple adopted Jaycee as a baby. From everything I've learned, they were decent people, although absent a lot because of their jobs. Jaycee's birth parents belong to Santorini elite families. One family has crime roots. There are lots of society parties and skiing trips in the winter. I don't have proof, but I think Jaycee might've visited them after her husband died. She mentioned the Greek family to me, told me she intended heading there for Christmas."

"Did Jaycee leave decent savings? A nest egg for Kian?" Saber asked.

"She had investments, but she ran through a lot of cash paying medical bills. She left money for Kian's education."

"So we assume that whoever you've spotted lurking around is part of Jaycee's blood family?" Leo asked. "And since someone murdered Jaycee, it's Kian they want."

"That's the way my thoughts are headed. She always smelled of a fae/human mix to me, but it wasn't anything we discussed. I kept my secrets close, and Jaycee did the same until she gave me access to the personal papers she kept for Kian. Jaycee's husband was a snow leopard shifter. Either Jaycee disclosed Kian's location before she died, or this man inherited the same tracking abilities as Jaycee. Perhaps the answer is the obvious one. Jaycee's newfound family is aware Kian is a shifter and wishes to profit from this info."

"Not while we're watching over him," Saber snapped. "If they want Kian, the shifter, that means a large percentage of Middlemarch children are in danger."

"We need to bring in Henry with his dogs and Laura and Charlie," Leo said.

"As much as I loathe the idea, it might be easiest if we set a trap," Isabella said slowly. Her fingernails dug into her palms, the idea hateful even if it was a practical one.

The two brothers shared a glance before Saber spoke. "Let's leave that as a last resort. Our volunteers will meet at the police station. We'll divide the town and patrol for the next few nights.

Leo, you and Isabella should behave as normal and stay with Kian after tonight. You can protect him and yourselves. We'll be available too."

"Damn straight. We'll protect Kian. Jaycee gave him to Isabella, which means he's ours now. Kian is our son," Leo snapped. "And we're not about to let someone kidnap him."

Pride and love surged in Isabella, and she reached for Leo's hand. She squeezed it tightly, trying to convey everything she'd experienced on hearing his words of claiming and acceptance. "Kian is ours, and we will protect him with everything we have."

Saber flashed them a sudden grin. "Despite the horrid situation, parenting looks good on both of you."

"Thanks," Isabella said. "I agree with your plan. This guy will expect us to be with Kian since we live here. What he doesn't know is we have special talents. If he tries to hurt Kian, I will gut him," she added fiercely.

Leo wrapped his arm around her waist. "Steady there, Mama Bear. Save that for later. Did you call the detective?"

"No, I'll do that now."

As she rang the detective and spoke to him, Saber clapped Leo on the shoulder and left. Five minutes later, she completed her call.

"Anything new?" Leo asked.

"The cops have hit a dead-end, although they found camera footage from a twenty-four-hour food store near the hospice. Not a clear visual. The man wore a cap to obscure his face. He walked toward the hospice around the time of Jaycee's death. Tall and fit, wearing dark clothing. Gave the impression it was a man. The nurse described a similar figure."

"That's it?"

"Yeah. I mentioned we'd had someone loitering around our house and, given Jaycee's murder, we'd contacted the local police. Although he didn't say it, this worried the detective. He told me this murder had hit his team hard, and the knowledge of a child's involvement made it worse."

"Isabella, we'll protect Kian," Leo said. "We have the advantage because this person won't know we're shifters."

Leo's physical touch helped to quash the worst of her fears. Kian was safe for now, and she had to believe either she or one of their friends would catch this stranger and force the truth from him.

Hours later, Isabella sank onto the edge of their bed and pulled off her socks. They'd checked every bed-and-breakfast, the camping ground, the hotel, and rental properties in the vicinity. They'd prowled the streets, keeping to the shadows and sniffing for the stranger's scent. She, Leo, and Saber had checked myriad trails on the road and come up empty. Now, it was three in the morning, and they'd retreated to their homes for rest.

"I should do more. And I have this urge to reassure myself Kian is safe."

"Gut instinct?" Leo asked, his tone sharp.

Isabella's shoulders slumped. "No, I've become attached to him. He's a terrific kid and considering everything that has happened in his short life, he's doing remarkably well."

"I've fallen in love with the little man too," Leo said. "Come on. Into bed with you. Neither of us will be much good for Kian if we don't sleep."

Isabella hauled off her remaining clothes and stretched out with a happy sigh. Leo flicked off the bedside lamp, plunging the room into darkness.

"Which Christmas function is next?" Leo murmured. "What have you, Emily, and Tomasine arranged for the kids next week?"

Isabella pressed close to Leo, needing his silent strength to recharge her reserves. "We were going on a picnic to the river if the weather stays nice, and apart from that, we'd intended to drop them off at the morning craft classes. If we could, I'd like to keep the routine normal, and Kian enjoys making things. He has a talent for art."

"I'd noticed. That shouldn't be a problem. We'll arrange for two men to hang around and offer added security. What about Christmas stuff?"

"Nothing until next week when we have the Christmas fair."

"Hopefully, this will be over by then," Leo murmured, an enormous yawn escaping.

For the next few days, everyone jumped at any foreign sound. Around town, there was much guarding and heightened security, although the local humans didn't appear to notice. It was nerve-racking, and Isabella hated every moment. She preferred to face danger head-on instead of waiting for it to skulk into prominence. This delay was working on her last nerve and destroying her patience.

Today, they were taking the kids on a picnic, escorted by Henry and his dogs and Leo. With Isabella present and Tomasine and Sylvie, there were enough adults to watch the kids and repel any interlopers who might crash their party. Isabella kind of wished their quarry would appear, so this would end, and they could enjoy the run-up to Christmas without constant glances over their shoulders.

It didn't happen, but the kids had a grand time splashing and receiving a swimming lesson in the calm rock pool formed by a recent flood. Kian swam like a fish, naturally doing everything Leo and the others instructed.

"They're all instinctive swimmers," Tomasine said. "Not surprising given their feline genes."

When Isabella paid closer attention to the other kids, she saw it was true. Leo loved to swim. Her—not so much because of her chameleon shifter characteristics. Sudden cold could debilitate her, and this was a vulnerability she kept close.

Her attention returned to Kian. He'd shifted and was swimming like a champ, looking so cute in his kittenish form, she couldn't find it in herself to growl at him. She scanned the area—one they'd chosen for its privacy.

"He's fine," Tomasine said. "My boys are envious of his ability to shift, especially since they know Sylvie shifted at their age." She pulled a face. "Sylvie told them they were defective, and Felix and I might trade them in for other more accomplished shifter kids."

"That's not like Sylvie."

"Oh, the boys deserved it. They'd gone into Sylvie's room and poked through her possessions. They also played with her makeup and decimated

MY PRECIOUS GIFT

it. Felix fitted a lock for her since my hellions have poked where they shouldn't before."

"Haven't they heard curiosity killed the cat?"

"Ha! In punishment, they're giving Sylvie half of their pocket money each week so she can purchase new makeup. Um, don't tell Sylvie, but I took photos." Tomasine glanced guiltily at her daughter, where she was helping with the swimming lessons. She pulled out her phone, scrolled, and handed it to Isabella.

A half-laugh escaped Isabella since the two brothers were wearing high-heels. They'd covered their faces with bright splashes of makeup, and one carried a plastic bow with rubber-tipped arrows while the other wee boy carried a silver pistol. "Ah, why the shoes?"

"I asked, but their answer made no sense—" Tomasine broke off, her gaze focused on a tree copse over the river.

"Nine o'clock across the water. I spotted a flash of light or a reflection."

"Henry must've spotted it too," Isabella said, staring in the direction Tomasine had signaled. She stood and walked toward Kian, who was now in his human form. "Time for everyone to get out. We're going to the café for ice cream. Everyone get dressed." She plucked Kian off his feet. *"Broom! Broom!"*

The boy's laughter rang out as Isabella whirled him through the air. She set him on his feet and spoke to him in a low voice while she dried him with a bright orange-and-red beach towel. "Kian, someone is watching us from the trees across the river. Please stay in two legs."

A tiny pucker appeared between his eyes. "Watching?"

"Yes, we're hunting him, but you must remain with the other children and keep each other safe." She wasn't confident he understood, despite his solemn nod. "No more four legs unless Leo or I tell you it's okay."

He nodded again, and Isabella whisked a dry lime-green T-shirt over his head. She made a mental note to contact the detective in Melbourne again since she hadn't touched base for several days. She'd have to be content with that and continue to monitor Kian and their surroundings.

"What is your favorite ice cream?" she asked Kian. "I don't know, and I think I should."

His forehead scrunched as he thought, then the wrinkles magically cleared.

"All ice cream," he said.

And that, Isabella thought, was a perfectly delightful and sensible answer. A grin twitched her mouth, and by habit, she held it in restraint before deciding not to hide her feelings with Kian. In the past, she'd concealed her emotions, barricaded her thoughts behind an impassive mask. Leo had pushed past her self-imposed walls, as had Tomasine and Leo's brothers and their wives. She trusted them and allowed them to see the real Isabella. Kian was her responsibility now. *Her son. Leo's son.* He should have everything she'd wished for as a kid and had never received from her feckless parents.

Jaycee's son deserved nothing but the best.

Chapter 16

A Café Visit

Isabella and the other adults dried off the kids and herded them to their vehicles while Henry took his dogs across the river to investigate. Ten minutes later, they piled out of the farm vehicles and entered Storm in a Teacup, the kids clamoring for ice cream.

"I'll help Emily if you watch Kian," Isabella suggested.

"Take Sylvie with you," Tomasine said. "Leo and I can corral the kids. We'll be out in the garden."

Isabella grabbed Sylvie, and they rounded the counter to offer their services to a red-faced and stressed Emily.

"You should've rung. Either Tomasine or I could've come back to help," Isabella chided. "Why don't I take over the front counter and coffee making? You sit with Tomasine and have a rest while Sylvie organizes ice cream for the kids."

"Ramsay needs help with the baking," Emily protested.

"I'll do it," Sylvie piped up, her brown eyes flashing eagerness. "I want to learn more of his tips and tricks."

Isabella made shooing motions with her hands. "Go. Rest."

Isabella checked on Kian twice, but Leo was there, and she had confidence he'd protect Kian with his life if necessary.

Henry arrived, giving Isabella a shake of his blond head when he strode past the counter to join Leo and Tomasine. Disappointment surged through her. This waiting was wearing on everyone.

The afternoon passed in a blur since Isabella stayed to work in the café while Leo took Kian home and later met up with Saber and Felix to muster sheep. She arrived home before Leo and Kian and had steak, salad, and potatoes ready for them as soon as they washed up.

"How did you enjoy the muster?" Isabella asked.

"Had to stay in two legs." Kian sounded disgruntled.

"I explained that," Leo said, an edge to his voice.

Isabella grinned down at her steak. "Did you get all the sheep?"

"Yes," Leo said. "Kian is a natural tracker."

A lightbulb switched on in Isabella. "Kian, the man who ran away with you—what did he smell like? Did you detect him this week?"

Kian popped a too-big piece of steak into his mouth and chewed with relish, his sharp teeth making quick work of the meat. He swallowed. Frowned. "Like Mama, but more..." He hesitated, struggling to describe the scent.

Isabella exchanged a glance with Leo.

"Like dirt? Metal? Water?" Leo ran through other scents, but Kian shook his head.

"Have you smelled him this week?" Isabella repeated.

Kian picked up another enormous piece of meat.

"No, Kian." Isabella took the steak from him and placed it back on his plate, ignoring Kian's snarl of displeasure because he feared she was stealing his food. "Like this," she said, demonstrating how to cut up his meat. "You try now."

He stared at her with unblinking blue eyes before finally attempting to copy. A piece of steak flew across the table before he cut the meat into smaller pieces.

"Excellent job," Isabella said.

"Kian," Leo said. "Have you smelled the man here?"

"Yes," Kian said.

Frustration bubbled in Isabella, but she tamped it down. He was a child, and everything in his world had shifted when his mother had left him on their doorstep. They—*she*—needed to exercise patience.

Leo must've come to a similar decision because he said, "If you smell him again, can you tell Isabella or me?"

"Yes." Kian finished his steak and curled his lip at the salad. He showed more interest in the potato but poked his fork at the green chive garnish, clear suspicion in his expression.

"Just try," Isabella said, taking care to modulate her tone. "You need to sample many foods, even the green ones. A balanced diet—that means when you eat foods that are different colors—will help you turn into a stronger snow leopard."

"When Saber and Felix and I were your age, our mother made us try everything. Even the green stuff," Leo said. "It had to have chew marks on it to show we'd tried it. Most of it tastes better than it looks."

Kian appeared doubtful, but Isabella was pleased to see he had tried everything on his plate by the end of the meal. She'd take that as a win.

The following day, Leo took Kian to the vineyard while Isabella headed to the café. She kept busy serving on the counter, making coffee, and delivering drinks and food to customers. The ready-to-go attitude that she'd worn like a cloak during her assassin days had returned. Every noise had her whipping to attention, her gaze shifting left and right and scrutinizing every stranger.

Emily and Ramsay spent the morning baking dozens and dozens of cookies and gingerbread for the Christmas evening fair. The Feline Council had gone all out, organizing strolling singers, drinks and food stalls, Christmas crafts for sale, and a Santa grotto. One of the older council members, Sid, was even reading *A Christmas Carol*—a condensed version, especially for the town's children.

Today, there were a lot of visitors in town. Some came from a cruise ship, currently berthed in Dunedin, while others were in Middlemarch to see family for the festive holidays. Isabella scanned faces and cataloged scents of the strangers automatically as she worked. Not a single customer stood out as objectionable or suspect. Other than the demanding woman with three giggling teenage girls in tow. Isabella gave her some slack since she'd dealt with Edwina and Suzie and barely survived with an intact temper.

Almost as if she'd conjured them, the two teens sailed into the café with a male escort. He must be a family friend since he was teasing the girls with old familiarity. They settled at a table and cast a glance in her direction as if waiting for table service. Although Emily preferred customers to come to the counter to order, she was adaptable.

Another large group entered the café, bringing a wash of dry grassy heat and artificial perfume.

"Sylvie, can you take Edwina and Suzie's order while I deal with this group?" Isabella asked in a low voice.

Sylvie pulled a face. "Do I have to? They don't like me ever since Jamie snubbed them in favor of spending time with me."

Sympathy gripped Isabella. Sylvie and Jamie had been close friends until he'd left to attend university in Auckland. "Please do me this favor. You might save me from murder charges."

Sylvie laughed. "Just this once. It's your turn next time they come into the café. You'd think they'd get the hint."

"Their tenacity is baffling," Isabella agreed. She smiled at the hovering customers. "Hello. Welcome to Storm in a Teacup. Are you paying together or separately?"

"Do we sit down?" a busty woman asked in a strong American accent.

"You order with me and pay, I give you a number, and you find an empty seat either here or outside in the garden.

"Is there shade out there?" a thin woman asked, her accent less pronounced. "I can't believe y'all don't have air conditioning."

Isabella had heard this before and merely widened her smile and waited. When they continued to dither, she prompted them, "Who would like to order first?"

Sylvie came back and slipped an order note near the coffee machine. "I'll take over if you want to start on the coffee."

"Thanks."

Isabella and Sylvie worked non-stop all morning. They cleared tables and made sandwiches and rolls for the cabinet between customers. It was only after the lunch rush when the stream of customers slowed that Isabella quizzed Sylvie.

"Were Edwina and Suzie rude to you?"

Sylvie grimaced. "No more than usual. I think they were trying to impress the man with them. They make flirtation into a competition. Must've used a lot of calories fluttering their eyelashes. So much mascara! It must've been like lifting weights."

A half-laugh, half-snort escaped Isabella. "Did he flirt back?"

"Yes, and no. He was asking questions about the café and the town when I arrived to take their order. He was a human."

Isabella couldn't conjure the man's face. No, he'd kept it angled away from her. "Can you describe the man?"

"No," Sylvie said slowly. "When I arrived, he excused himself and left to go to the restrooms."

"What about when you took them their coffee and food?"

"That time, he left briefly to make a phone call," Sylvie said.

Their gazes met, and they swung around, but Edwina, Suzie, and their male guest had left long ago.

"I'll check for a scent," Isabella said.

"Isabella." Sylvie stayed Isabella with a quick hand on her shoulder. "I sanitized the table and chairs as per our normal procedure. Sorry."

"I'll try, anyway." It proved to be an exercise in frustration. Given the number of customers, tracking anyone from the café was impossible.

Isabella strode out the back into the kitchen to call Leo.

"Sweetheart," he said.

"A man was hanging out with Edwina and Suzie. It might be nothing, but he avoided Sylvie and me. Neither of us glimpsed his face. We've had a lot of customers, so tracking him will be impossible." She paused, recalling the threesome to mind. "He's wearing a navy-blue T-shirt. It had writing in white on the front, but I didn't read the slogan or advertising. Light-colored shorts. I didn't see his footwear. He had black hair and stood around six feet. Build." She wrinkled her nose as she replayed the scene. "Best I can say is average. Neither overweight nor thin. Sylvie, can you add any details?"

"He possesses a slight medical scent as if he'd used hand sanitizer or something similar. He wore sunglasses. Black ones with reflective lenses. He is vain about his hair because he'd had it professionally cut recently, and he wore hair product that reminded me of an orchard. Not citrus, but something fruity."

Isabella nodded at Sylvie with approval. "Excellent job. Did you get that, Leo?"

"Yeah. I'm with Saber. We'll let you know our plan of attack."

"It might be nothing," Isabella said. "But it seems strange he made certain that neither Sylvie nor I saw his face. Edwina and Suzie will know more. I could beat it out of them."

Saber spoke in the background as Leo spluttered out a laugh.

"No, you can't," Leo said once he'd regained composure. "You need to set a good example since you're a parent now."

"You haven't had several run-ins with those two she-cats. They're arrogant and full of themselves, and I worry about their future. A whoppin' might make them rethink their path."

"Doubt it," Sylvie said. "Leo, buy Isabella a punching bag for Christmas. I can paint caricatures of Edwina and Suzie to paste on it."

That witticism sent both Leo and Saber into laughter, and the titters coming from Emily and guffaw from Ramsay had Isabella quelling them with a fierce scowl.

"That does it," Isabella said, lifting her nose into the air. "You're all off my Christmas card list. Leo: spare room." Isabella hung up to another round of laughter.

"What's happening?" Emily asked. As the only human in the group, she sometimes missed information since her hearing wasn't as good as theirs.

"A man visited the café with Edwina and Suzie. It might have been innocent, but his behavior was odd. Saber and Leo are on the job."

"At least the kids are together and safe," Emily said. "My girls were so excited to visit Henry and learn about training puppies. Gerard and London were helping Henry. With that many kids, he'll need the backup."

Isabella silently agreed about Henry's security since it was his profession. Even so, it was as if a stopwatch had clicked on inside her, and it was rapidly ticking. To what, Isabella wasn't sure. All she knew was she had a bad feeling.

Damn shame, her instincts hadn't screamed at her when the man had waltzed into Storm in a Teacup.

"Edwina and Suzie distracted me. Somehow, this guy knew and used this information to enter. If he'd watched the place, he'd know that Kian wasn't here," she said.

"Isabella, he's a human," Sylvie said. "We have the advantage. If he's intent on snatching Kian, it mightn't have occurred to him there are more shifters."

Isabella confirmed her agreement with a curt nod. All true, but that didn't stop the ticking of her damn internal clock.

Chapter 17

Christmas Fair

The predicted rain detoured around Otago and slammed into the Southern Alps instead, which meant their Christmas fair took place on a balmy summer evening. A gentle breeze took the sting out of the day's heat, and as the sun slid lower toward the hills, the fairy lights blinked to life, spreading a magical ambiance across the hastily erected stalls and tents on the main street of Middlemarch.

Giant Christmas baubles decorated each lamppost, and they shone with blue and white lights of their own, while the giant red-and-white striped candy canes and bows of red and green decorated the town's Christmas tree.

Isabella clutched one of Kian's hands while Leo walked a half step behind them, his attentive gaze flicking left and right. At least, Isabella assumed Leo was doing the same as she was. He placed a hand on her tense shoulder, and she jumped, even though she recognized his touch.

"Steady," he said. "You're quivering like a firecracker about to explode."

"My instincts failed me when that man came into the store with Edwina and Suzie, but everything we've learned tells me this is the guy. He'll strike tonight."

"We're ready for him. All of us."

When Isabella turned to watch his face, she noted the curl of distaste on his lips.

"How will the council punish those she-cats?" Isabella asked. "Although they didn't blab feline secrets, they handed Kian on a plate, telling the man how he suddenly appeared, and everyone in the Mitchell family is tight-lipped about his origins. The she-cats blurted everything they knew and embellished it, trying to impress him." She fantasized about wringing their necks and clenched her free hand so hard her knuckles cracked. "Those girls should stay away from me."

Leo tensed, and immediately Isabella's muscles went taut with alarm. Her hand tightened on Kian's, and he cried in protest.

"Sorry, sweetie," she said and squatted to reassure him. "Would you like to try a piece of gingerbread? It's spicy."

When he frowned in confusion, she explained. "Spicy means it might be hot on your tongue. Your tongue and mouth might tingle even though the food is in your tummy." She poked his belly in illustration.

"Try now," he said.

"He's adventurous with food—way more than us at the same age," Leo said.

Isabella straightened. "Why are you so tense?"

"Edwina and Suzie are prowling in our direction."

Isabella whirled around to survey the crowd and spotted the teens. Both girls wore short denim skirts and revealing, clingy tops that left little to the imagination. Their high-heel shoes, which they handled as if they were extensions of their body, made them much taller than the group of brothers and sisters that swarmed around them. Isabella glared at the pair, so angry she quivered with her fury.

"Steady," Leo said. "You can't make a scene."

"No, but I can email a letter of complaint to the Feline Council and demand an apology and restitution. I will take action because their stupidity deserves consequences. What they have done is thoughtless and reprehensible. I cannot forgive them."

"There's Saber," Leo said, gesturing to their right. "He and Emily and the girls are right beside the gingerbread stall. Isabella, sweetheart, I'm as angry as you, and I will sign my name to that letter of yours. This time, those two girls won't skate away without punishment. Edwina and Suzie knew better, yet because you irked them, they misplaced their commonsense."

Kian squeezed her hand, his button nose quivering and his blue eyes beseeching. With his tawny hair and darker splotchy undertones, the boy drew attention. Humans and shifters alike smiled at him. Locals said hello and their children—the shifter ones—politely sniffed and smiled with Kian aping their actions.

They wove through the crowd toward Saber and Emily, their progress slow given the large turnout. Isabella kept Kian's hand gripped tightly in hers and didn't release it until they reached their family. To her surprise, Kian grasped it again and tugged for her attention.

"Spicy food," he said, cocking his head as he stared up at her.

"I'm buying gingerbread," Isabella said. "Anyone else want a piece?"

"I love it," Emily said. "Saber and the girls aren't fans."

"Buy two," Leo suggested. "We'll share with Emily."

Isabella nodded and turned to Ramsay, who was waiting to take their order. His two assistants were busy serving other customers.

"It's been busy," Ramsay said when Isabella handed over a ten-dollar note. "I thought I'd cooked surplus cookies and gingerbread. Luckily, I listened to Emily."

Isabella privately thought he might be the attraction since most customers were young women—shifter and human. Yet Ramsey displayed no reaction apart from professional courtesy and a friendly smile. He'd had a tough childhood but had found a home here in Middlemarch when he wasn't at his apprentice cooking gig in Dunedin.

"If this gingerbread tastes as good as it smells, it's no wonder you're doing a brisk trade," she said.

Leo and Kian drifted with his brother, and she caught up with them at the face-painting corner. The two girls and Kian sat on chairs, and three women skillfully spread paint across their cheeks.

"Kian has a crush," Leo murmured, his amusement glinting in his pretty green eyes. "The woman suggested a cat face, and he demanded a wolf like Henry."

"Oh," Isabella said. "Did he understand he shouldn't mention cats and wolves to anyone?"

"She's human. She laughed and assured Kian she'd paint a wolf," Leo said.

"Has anyone seen this guy loitering around the place?" Isabella asked Saber. She kept her voice low so none of the children could hear.

"He has disappeared. No one has noticed him hovering in the background. His vanishing act is bothering me," Saber admitted. "I'm going to push for security cameras in the main street, at least. Given the graffiti fiasco and other incidents, the Feline Council needs to take this seriously."

"An excellent time to push," Isabella said in a tart voice. "Agnes and Valerie must feel torn, given their granddaughters' behavior and their positions on the council."

"Just what I was thinking," Saber said.

The face painters finished, and Kian beamed when the woman showed him his reflection in her mirror.

"That was a great idea," Isabella said. "It's harder to recognize Kian with the face paint."

"Leo's idea," Saber said.

"All right," Emily said to the kids. "Let's take a photo. Kian, do you want to stand between the two cats?"

"Woof," Kian said without warning, making everyone laugh.

Isabella took several photos with her phone, as did Emily before Isabella handed Kian a piece of gingerbread. He took an eager bite, his eyes widening. Isabella thought he might spit it out, but he swallowed and grinned before taking another larger bite.

"You're so lucky," Emily said. "My girls won't eat any vegetables, and they refuse to try new meals without sniffing every bite. It's embarrassing. We can't take them to a restaurant."

"His mother did this. I can't take any credit," Isabella replied. "Where to next?"

A group of roving carolers strolled up to them and sang about dancing around the Christmas tree. The singers wore costumes: black suits with top hats for the men while the woman had donned long dresses with hoops and petticoats. Flower-festooned bonnets perched on their heads. Kian skipped toward the quintet with a shout of excitement. He enjoyed music and art and seemed physically unable to remain still when he heard a rhythmic beat. Perhaps they could investigate

MY PRECIOUS GIFT

music lessons. Something to consider. He bopped to the song and clapped in delight once the carol ended.

The carolers held out a bucket. Confusion wrinkled Kian's nose, and he frowned at her and Leo with a what-the-heck expression. Leo chuckled and joined Kian. He handed him several coins and crouched beside the boy to show he should toss them into the bucket. Kian dropped them with a clunk, and the coins rattled against the others already donated by passersby.

"Let's wander," Isabella said, although her enthusiasm lacked. Her stomach quivered, and she had to force the tension from her limbs.

· ♥ · ♥ · ♥ · ♥ · ♥ ·

Concern rose in Leo. Apprehension stretched Isabella tight and she jumped at each unfamiliar noise. Worse, her jitters were extending to Kian. He was swiveling his head and testing the air, identifying him as feline to anyone who understood the signs.

"Isabella, you're frightening the lad," Leo murmured against her ear, keeping his voice soft so as not to reach Kian.

Her shoulders slumped before she relaxed against him. "I can't help it. Jaycee hovers in my mind, and my nerves and worry grows. The last thing I want is him injured under my watch. I owe it to Jaycee to do my best work on this assignment. She counted on me." She paused. "I've become attached to Kian."

"You love him, as do I, but you're putting too much pressure on yourself. Kian is a cheerful kid. He's mostly well-behaved, and Jaycee has given him excellent survival skills. We're all watching out for him." The strain in her expression had Leo's heart twisting. Some considered his mate a haughty woman with no feelings. Not true. She experienced everything deeply but had learned to hide behind a mask. He loved her, and gradually his constant love and presence had melted her outer protective layer. This situation with Kian had thrown her. He'd known, without a discussion, she keenly felt the lack of a child, and when well-meaning but nosy old biddies demanded to know when she and Leo were having children, his heart had bruised and ached for her.

Her inability to bear children hurt Isabella and Kian's arrival in their lives had provided an opportunity for her to step into the role she'd always craved. The abruptness had thrown her, but he had every confidence in his mate. Even though she kept second-guessing herself, she bore an enormous heart and would do anything for friends or family. Anything, including killing and burying the body.

"Where to next?" Leo asked, offering Kian and Isabella a bright smile.

"The toy stall!" Saber's girls shrieked together. They darted past Kian, Olivia grabbing for Kian's hand and dragging him after her.

Saber laughed ruefully and strolled after the children, leaving Emily, Leo, and Isabella to follow.

"No one has seen anything out of the ordinary," Leo whispered. "Try to enjoy the night. The weather is perfect, and we should have fun and stuff ourselves full of Christmas treats. See the stall selling peppermint sticks? Why don't I buy one to put in Kian's Christmas stocking?"

Emily grasped Isabella's arm but didn't appear to notice Isabella's stress. "I'm off to check out dresses. I want a new Christmas outfit, and work has cut into shopping trips. Caroline promised she'd hold back garments she thought I might like."

"Yes, okay." Isabella nodded and even managed a smile. "I'll check out the books on the stall next to the toys. Saber is supervising the kids."

"Go with Emily and buy yourself a new dress for Christmas too," Leo said, giving her a gentle shunt after Emily. "Saber and I have got this."

Isabella sent him a searching glance before dipping her head in a brief nod.

"Buy something sexy," Leo said. "Does Caroline have kid's clothes? You could get a shirt for Kian. Maybe something Christmassy. We could start a family tradition, and all wear Christmas-themed T-shirts or, for the women, dresses. Suggest it to Emily when you catch up with her and tell me later if she approves of the idea."

Leo watched Isabella hesitate, then stride away to chase after her sister-in-law. He joined Saber, and they watched the kids exploring the toys. Kian headed straight to the stuffed toys and the plush wolf.

He sniffed it, poked and prodded at the toy animal before marching to Leo and holding it out. "Mine," he said.

Remembering an earlier discussion between Saber and Emily about not spoiling kids, Leo tapped his chin. "How about this for a deal? I'll buy the wolf for you, but you have to help Isabella set the table for breakfast and dinner and keep your room tidy in exchange."

Bright intelligence shone in Kian's eyes. He understood what Leo required of him and nodded, holding the wolf out to Leo.

"Mine," he repeated.

"All right," Leo agreed. "I'll tell Isabella about your end of the deal when we get home."

"Yes," Kian said, squaring his tiny shoulders.

When Leo rose to his full height, Saber reached over and squeezed his arm.

"Well done, bro. You're a natural."

Leo huffed out a breath, although pride and pleasure wrapped around him at Saber's compliment. "Half the time—hell, *all* the time I'm winging it because I have no clue."

"You and Isabella are doing a fantastic job. If you need advice, please ask. We all started with limited knowledge, and we improvise most of the time. Understand that kids are ferocious beasts. If you show fear, they step all over you."

Leo gawked at Saber, convinced his brother was joking.

"I'm not kidding," Saber said. "You ask Emily. Babysitting is different because you can give the kids back, but when they misbehave and make you want to pull out your hair and shout, you can't. Outsmart them with brains. Most of us have had the same problems, which is why I'm telling you to seek advice. It's what Felix and I do when we're having issues. Welcome to the club."

Bemused, Leo merely nodded and pulled out his wallet to purchase the stuffed wolf for Kian. A thought occurred, and once he'd secured the toy and handed it to a delighted Kian.

"Saber, once we finish here, can we find Henry? Does he have any pups left in his recent litter?"

"Ah," Saber said, glancing at Kian with understanding. "See, you're thinking like a parent already. That would be a perfect gift to help him settle into Middlemarch. They could grow together." He checked on his twins. "Girls, you have five minutes to pick one toy each."

Kian stood beside Leo, holding his plush toy carefully and crooning to it in soft purrs that most wouldn't hear. Leo did and smiled at the contented sounds. A noisy squabble broke out between Saber's girls, and Leo pulled a face. Compared to Saber's twins, Kian was much easier.

Leo watched with interest while a decisive Saber refereed.

"Olivia. Sophia. Girls, if you don't cease your bickering, neither of you will receive a toy. I will take you home. You will miss the marching band, the lolly scramble, and Santa."

MY PRECIOUS GIFT

The twins fell silent, slid glares like daggers at each other, and stood mutinous.

Saber waited them out, and when the girls continued their glowers, he sighed. "That's it. No toys. We'll find your mother."

Leo fell into step with Saber, nudging Kian to walk in front of him while they wandered to the next aisle of stalls. The girls spoke in fierce whispers behind them, and Leo caught Saber's eye roll. Leo spotted Henry just as they reached Caroline's dress stall.

"Henry is over there with Gerard and London," Leo said.

Saber nodded. "I'll watch Kian while you chat with Henry. If the twins keep this up, I'm taking them home, but I'll leave either Emily or Isabella in charge of Kian. Okay?"

"Perfect." Leo checked on Kian, who still cooed to his toy wolf. Isabella was chatting with Caroline. Reassured his family was okay, he left to speak with Henry.

When he arrived back at the dress stall, Saber and the twins had gone. Emily and Isabella were still with Caroline and held cloth bags with Caroline's emblem decorating the outside. Satisfaction filled Leo. Isabella seldom spent money on herself, despite the healthy fortune she'd amassed over the years.

He glanced around for Kian and frowned when the boy was nowhere in sight. Long strides took Leo to Isabella and Emily.

The brass band started their slow, ponderous march down the street, and the locals cheered. The band had improved since their first outing six months ago, and their proud swagger along the main road showed they knew it.

Leo had already learned how much Kian loved music. Had the boy run to march along behind them? He checked faces, dragged in scents.

"Isabella, I can't find Kian," Leo said, panic roaring through him.

Fear shot across her face, and they clutched each other. Both scanned the crowds, searching for the small boy holding his toy wolf.

"Where did you see him last?" Saber asked, arriving back with his daughters. His sharp tone forced Leo to pull himself together.

"When we purchased the toy wolf."

"He was right with me," Isabella said, her voice distraught. She blamed herself.

Leo clasped her hand and squeezed in silent commiseration.

"We'll find him," Saber said, his manner calm. "We'll split up and each search a section of the fair."

The alarm racing through Leo almost took him out at the knees. When he glanced at Isabella, tears welled in her eyes, and that made Leo feel worse.

"Isabella. Leo, it's not your fault," Saber said. "Kids are fast, and they get excited at events like this. They see a shiny object and have to get closer. You search this side of the street and alert anyone you see to help. I'll search the other side." Saber strode away, his gaze swinging from side to side as he cataloged faces.

"The girls and I will search around here," Emily said, shepherding her twins in front of her.

Leo nodded, a sense of numbness taking over.

"I'm so sorry, Leo," Isabella said, her cheeks pale. "He was here minutes ago."

"It's not your fault. Remember when Tomasine's boys wandered off? You know what kids are like and how bad we felt when we lost them in that Dunedin department store," Leo said. "Come on. Let's find Kian."

Leo strode away, checking every child's face. He ran into Charlie and his two mates and asked if they'd seen Kian. They hadn't but joined the hunt.

Half an hour later, he and Isabella met Saber and Emily and the growing group of friends and family who'd joined the search party.

No one had spotted Kian, and now worry and panic truly set in.

"We'll search farther afield," Laura said, wearing her cop-face. "Extend the search grid. What was he wearing?"

"He was wearing a green T-shirt with a frog on the front, brown shorts, and sandals," Isabella said. "His face is painted like a wolf."

"He was carrying a toy wolf. I bought it for him tonight," Leo added.

"Right," Laura said and organized everyone.

Leo jumped when Isabella pressed close, then after glimpsing her face, he hauled her against his chest.

"What if we can't find him, Leo?" She gave an audible swallow. "I can't fail Jaycee or Kian."

"We'll find him."

Leo clasped her hand, and after a quick word with Laura, he and Isabella strode along the street, running parallel to Middlemarch's main one. As one, they halted to inhale.

"Kian's scent," Isabella said, alert and more herself now.

Leo pulled out his phone and called Laura, telling him of the fresh development while Isabella followed the trail.

Farther down the street, at the next intersection, something lay on the road. Leo recognized it instantly. "That's Kian's wolf!"

Chapter 18

Got Him!

He'd spent the last week in this hick town, waiting to get his chance to grab the kid. These people shouldn't have Kian. If Jaycee had done the typical thing, he would've avoided this drama. He wouldn't have had to confront her in Melbourne.

Peter still wasn't sure how it had happened, but things had gone haywire, and he'd lost control of the situation.

Who knew a person contained that much blood?

Jaycee had laughed at him, called him weak when she was the one who resembled a stick figure. Right to the end, she'd clutched her secrets and refused to tell him a thing. He'd won, though, and now he was in for a huge payday.

A part of it was dumb luck.

He'd tracked down his newfound sister and hit her up for a loan. Hell, he hadn't realized she'd had a husband, let alone a child.

A kid who transformed into a leopard.

Immediately, he'd seen an escape from his money crisis. The bitch had refused to finance him, but this extraordinary knowledge had been a godsend.

How had she earned her wealth anyhow? She'd never told him that either.

Finding her had been easy, but after he'd left to make arrangements and research the best method to monetize his knowledge, the bitch had run. He'd tracked her for months before he'd discovered her in Melbourne.

But the boy hadn't been present, and Jaycee had refused to tell him what she'd done with the hellcat that had clawed his best trousers to hell. He'd thought he could force her with threats, but she'd laughed. Losing his temper had been stupid, but he'd discovered the information he'd wanted in the hospice records. Oh, he hadn't known the kid had been in the hick country town, but he'd hoped to find a clue to lead him to the child.

The kid wriggled and hissed and bit. Peter used his free hand to cuff the abomination over the head and give him a taste of what might happen if he refused cooperation.

The boy grew limp and dropped the stupid wolf toy he'd clung to so proudly. Peter caught his foot on the edge of a pothole and almost fell. He dropped the kid, and the boy thumped to the road and didn't move.

"Jaysus," he muttered, anxiety kicking him in the gut. Was the boy dead? Had he killed him? He hadn't hit him that hard. Peter crouched beside the boy and tested for a pulse. The even *thump, thump, thump* made him shaky with relief.

More confident now, he scooped the boy into his arms and strode toward his car. The sooner he escaped this dump, the better.

Luckily, the buyer had been so keen, he'd arranged to meet Peter in Auckland. All Peter needed to do was deliver Kian and collect his dough.

The only shame was Jaycee hadn't had more kids since a large portion of his prize would go to paying off his original debt. Bitch. She'd never given him a chance after their first meeting. His birth sister had rejected him. Pity she wasn't still alive so he could thumb his nose at her. He hadn't needed Jaycee. He'd managed on his own.

Peter reached his car and juggled Kian while he dug into his pockets for his keys. He unlocked the door, then moved to the rear. Kian came awake without warning. He snarled and swiped Peter in the face. The boy's hand was more cat than human, and his razor-sharp claws dug deep.

Peter yelped but didn't make the mistake of releasing his prize. Kian spat and snarled. He wriggled and thrashed.

"You can release him now," a harsh voice said from behind him.

The blonde woman Kian lived with stood before him, hands on her hips and fury on her face.

"Who's gonna make me?" he scoffed. "One blonde lady with attitude? I think not. Get out of my way. I'm taking my nephew."

"You're Kian's uncle. Jaycee's brother?" the blonde asked, openly gaping.

Enough of this. Peter thrust Kian into the car, but the boy had regained his senses and jumped at him before Peter could close and lock the door. Teeth gripped his arm and clamped down.

"Let him go," the woman ordered, plucking a weapon from her waistband.

The gun fired, and pain struck him seconds later. Peter screamed, the throb of his bitten arm and the searing agony in his foot almost taking him out at the knees.

"Don't make me tell you again," the blonde said. "Let Kian go."

"You can't shoot me," Peter snapped. "It's against the law."

The blonde laughed. "Taking my child is against the law too, but that didn't stop you from doing it."

"He's my nephew," Peter snapped. "You're no blood relative."

"Let him go."

"What? You're going to shoot me again?" Peter snapped.

"Yes," the blonde said sweetly. "I'll work my way up your body. Your knee next, I think."

"Isabella," a male called. "Where's Leo?"

"Positioning himself to get Kian," the blonde said.

A car door opened, and Peter whirled. "No!"

The gun fired, and pain exploded in his other foot, drawing his attention back to the woman. Belatedly, he realized she handled the gun like a pro, and confidence shimmered off her along with fiery determination.

Peter held out his hands, preparing to bluff his way through the situation and use his gift for bullshit. "Why don't we discuss this? Kian is my nephew. I'm Peter, Jaycee's brother. I intend to raise him as Jaycee would've wanted."

"Then why didn't you park in our front yard and knock on the door instead of creeping around to gather information about Leo and me?"

On the other side of the car, a soft voice murmured something Peter couldn't catch. *No!* He needed that kid.

"You know someone murdered your sister?" the woman demanded.

Peter jolted, an involuntary movement he tried to hide as he focused on the blonde. Judging by the condemnation in her eyes, he failed big time. It was the pain in his foot, both his feet.

Hell, what was he going to do? How did he escape this hick town with his nephew in tow? If he didn't arrive at the airport with the kid, the unscrupulous bastard waiting might decide Peter was superfluous. Even though he'd taken the precaution of keeping Kian's location to himself, Demetri had contacts. He had money. So much money.

Peter's thoughts raced like a hamster on a wheel as he attempted to fashion a plan. He was skilled at planning. His mother had always told him it was his strength since no matter how bad things got, he always circumnavigated danger.

This time was proving more difficult, but he still had the hidden talent he seldom used…

"Jaycee wanted me to raise Kian," he said with a slight smile. A smile meant to convey trustworthiness and confidence.

"Lie," the blonde said, her gaze hard with contempt. "She left him with me, along with the paperwork to make it legal. You want to call the cops. Do it." She glanced to her right. "Ah, here are the cops now. You can explain to them why you kidnapped Kian and scared him half to death." She glanced past him, silently communicating with someone else.

A couple, both dressed in shorts and T-shirts, flanked the blonde woman.

The woman groaned. "Did you shoot him, Isabella?"

The blonde shrugged. "He was escaping. I only shot him a bit."

The man snorted. "I can see his blood."

"But there isn't much." The blonde's expression turned thoughtful. "I don't think he's fully human, so watch him closely. Leo, is Kian hurt?"

"No, he seems okay. Kian, come back here." Urgency filled the man's voice.

Curious, Peter half-turned. He gathered his power, centering his mind and focusing in the way their father had taught him. It was harder for Peter, and a short flit knocked him on his arse for a good hour afterward, but if it meant he could escape and regroup, so be it.

"Kian!" the woman shouted.

MY PRECIOUS GIFT

Peter prepared to teleport into his car when something attached to his leg. Sharp teeth sucked away his concentration, and he flailed, trying to kick away the pain. It was Kian, and when Peter realized, he stopped fighting. Even better. He centered his mind, ready to teleport both himself and Kian into the car. He'd drive over these idiots and still make it to the airport in time for his flight.

A fierce growl rent the air, and a humongous black leopard slunk into view, followed by what looked like a big dog. No, a wolf! Both creatures were massive and bristled with fury. Peter stared, everything in him going still.

The wolf gave a sharp yip, and Kian retracted his claws and jumped away from Peter.

Peter tried to grab him, but the hissing kitten evaded his grasping hands and ran to stand between the leopard and wolf. Both animals retreated, with his freaky nephew wedged between them.

Damn.

But then inspiration hit, and the tiny seed grew to mammoth proportions. A black leopard. A werewolf. Were there more weirdos like Kian living in this country town?

Well, hello, fortune.

Now all he needed to do was save his skin and regroup. This was a tremendous opportunity waiting for him to make a plan.

He directed his focus as he never had, gloried as he felt the weightless sensation claim his body. The speechless blonde was the last thing he saw as he teleported.

Chapter 19

Handcuffs

"What the hell?" Isabella muttered. "Did you see that?"

"Did I see that arsehole blink out like something from a sci-fi movie?" Laura said, her voice heavy with disbelief. "Charlie, just when I think I'm getting a handle on this town's woo-woo shit, I'm blown away by a new revelation."

Isabella scowled, thinking of everything she'd learned from the dude. Peter. "Jaycee had crazy-good tracking skills, and I suspected fae blood even though she smelled human."

"Why didn't he pop in and grab Kian?" Leo demanded.

Isabella wrinkled her nose. "Limitations, maybe?"

"Even worse," Laura said. "Did you see his excitement when he spotted Gerard and Henry?"

"Yeah," Charlie said. "He's not going far. Whatever his plan, he's greedy for a larger payoff."

"I agree," Saber said, sliding from the shadows. "He'll be back, and he's a bigger danger than we presumed."

"He's injured, and we have his scent," Isabella said, her adrenaline spike slow to settle. The gun shook in her hand, and she secured the safety and slipped the weapon from sight. When she and Tomasine had fled Tomasine's crazy first husband, Isabella had thought she'd understood Tomasine's fear for her daughter, for her own life.

Isabella had been wrong. She hadn't understood at all. This bone-deep icy terror that slid through her veins dulled her capacity to think. She couldn't plan with her usual competence when panic for Kian threatened to bury her.

Leo placed his hand on her shoulder, seeming to understand she needed him. His touch grounded her, cleared the static in her brain.

"If the guy is a fairy, he should watch out," Isabella muttered. "I intend to stab him with a pin and fasten him on the top of my Christmas tree. That dude is not going anywhere."

Everyone stared then Laura snickered. "You did not say that," she said when she finally regained control.

"What? You don't think he deserves punishment?" Isabella demanded. "He stole Kian and intended to do something despicable with him. My bet is he was selling his nephew to the highest bidder. Now that he has seen Gerard and Henry, the dollar signs are flashing like billboards in his brain."

"He's on foot," Saber said. "My guess is he can't go far, otherwise why would he bother with a rental car? We need to search the town again, but this time, we lay a trap. Gerard. Henry. How would you like to play bait?"

Leo grasped Kian by the ruff and handed the boy his stuffed wolf. Kian released a loud purr before grabbing the precious toy in his teeth and toting the wolf over to Henry. Kian dropped the wolf in front of Henry's front paws and released a rumbly purr. Isabella watched the entire tableau with bemusement.

"Aw, that's sweet," Laura said.

"Kian likes Henry," Leo said with a smile.

"Let's move," Isabella said. "I'll take Kian and ask Tomasine and Emily to watch him. If they stay together in the middle of the crowd, he should be safe."

"No, stay with him," Leo said. "The rest of us have his scent. You protect Kian, and we'll hunt."

Isabella hesitated, then nodded. "Check the town buildings and surrounds. It's possible he teleported directly into a building."

"You take the streets to the west," Saber said to Gerard and Henry.

Both animals trotted away, noses to the ground as they tested for scents.

"Laura, Charlie," Saber said. "Can you search the building interiors? It will be easier for you than for us. Leo and I will take the east side. Everyone meet back at the café once you're finished."

"We'll escort you and Kian back to the Christmas fair," Leo said.

Isabella crossed to Kian. "Please shift, Kian." Then a problem presented itself. "Where are your clothes?"

Kian trotted toward the rental car and waited by the rear door.

"In there?" she asked him.

Kian yowled.

Isabella hurriedly opened the unlocked door. She spied Kian's green T-shirt immediately and picked it up. It bore a rip down the middle. His shorts had fared better since he'd slipped them off before his shift had claimed him. She handed him the brown shorts.

"Good job," she said. Given the circumstances, she couldn't blame Kian for ripping his clothes. "Quick, get dressed, and we'll get you another shirt. Caroline has a rack of boys' garments." Once Kian shifted, she helped him step into his shorts and draped the torn T-shirt over his shoulders. It would do for now. She took his hand and started walking back to the main street. As she walked, she constantly scanned faces. Emily had joined forces with Tomasine, and they were herding their excited kids to the edge of the street to stand with all the other children, awaiting the lolly scramble.

"Kian and I have backup," she said to Saber and Leo. "I have a tight grip on his hand, and he won't run off."

"Are you sure?" Leo asked.

"Positive."

Leo squeezed her biceps. "Stay safe. Both of you." The two brothers faded into the crowd.

The local fire brigade had geared up and perched on top of the fire engine. The driver honked the horn and proceeded at a crawl along the street while the firemen tossed handfuls of candy to the local kids. There was pushing and shoving. Shouts and screams as the children leaped on the wrapped sweets.

Kian tugged at her hand, his gaze imploring because he wanted to join the other kids.

She crouched, so she was his height. "Not today, okay? It's too dangerous. I promise we will have a lolly scramble at our next family party."

He stared at her before finally acquiescing. His shoulders drooped, but he nodded. Isabella rolled up to her full height, and they continued walking. She felt terrible as they stopped beside Emily and Tomasine.

"You found him," Emily said. "Where are the others?"

"Looking for Peter. That's his name. He's my friend's brother and Kian's uncle."

Emily gasped. "He's in the wind?"

"For the moment. He's tall and on the slender side. Five-nine or thereabouts. Styled short black hair with a touch of silver. Blue eyes. He was wearing black trousers and a black short-sleeved button-up. Oh, he might look a bit banged up. Kian scratched and bit to get free, and I shot his feet," Isabella reported.

Emily's eyes widened just as Kian stiffened at her side, his entire frame going rigid.

Isabella focused in the direction where Emily and Kian were staring and did a double-take. It was him, although he wouldn't spot her because of the dress racks.

She turned casually and shunted Kian between her and the dress rack. She plucked her phone from her pocket and speed-dialed Laura.

"Laura, he's in the main street, almost directly opposite Caroline's dress stall. He seems dazed and looks pale. My guess is the teleporting drained his energy. I'll call Saber and the others." She ended the call before Laura could reply. "Leo, across the road from Caroline's stall. Is Saber with you? Okay, I'll call him." She hung up again. She repeated the information before turning slowly to check on Peter. He still stood where she'd first glimpsed him. No one was paying him any attention, their interest focused on the kids scrambling to grab handfuls of candy.

Either he thought they couldn't touch him, or he was in trouble and couldn't move until he regained energy. No matter, because she didn't intend to let him escape. But what to do with Kian?

She crouched again, moving without haste. She placed a hand on each of Kian's shoulders. "Will you stay here with Tomasine and Emily so I can catch your uncle?"

He frowned.

"Leo and I need you to stay safe. We promised your mama we'd always keep you safe." She wasn't sure if he understood, but he nodded and moved a few steps to reach Emily. He clasped her hand, his big blue eyes solemn.

"Good boy," Emily said. "Once the twins get back with their stash, we'll confiscate some for you."

Kian grinned wide, displaying his sharp white teeth, and Isabella relaxed.

Reassured their boy was protected, Isabella slipped into hunting mode, ghosting through the crowd and using the mass of excited men, women, and children as barriers. She'd almost reached Peter when his head jerked upward. His gaze met hers, and she spotted the panic roaring through him. He took two tottering steps before Isabella tackled him, and they toppled. Peter grunted when he hit the ground. A woman screamed, and everyone in the vicinity scuttled back several steps as Isabella landed a solid punch.

"She's attacking that poor man," a man snapped. "Get her off him."

"She's hurting him," a woman cried.

"Is that blood?" another demanded. "Call the cops."

Peter struggled like a landed fish and tried to wriggle free. Isabella gripped him with determination, equally resolute not to let him escape.

"Stand back," Laura ordered, pushing through the crowd. The helpful citizens fell silent and stepped away from the melee.

Charlie sprinted behind Laura. They leaped on him and grabbed one of Peter's arms each.

Isabella peeled away and stood, dusting off her linen shorts and midnight blue silky tee.

"What's wrong with him?" Laura murmured in a low voice when they quickly subdued him. "Ugh, he's bleeding a lot."

"My guess is the teleporting sapped his energy. Kian mauled his legs when he tried to escape, and he has holes where I shot him." Satisfaction pulsed in her statement.

"We'll take him to the police station. Hopefully, he won't pop out of his cell before we can transport him to Australia for murdering his sister," Laura said.

Isabella lifted her chin. "He's not escaping again. I'm coming with you."

"How are we going to stop him vanishing again?" Charlie demanded. "We're not equipped to deal with magical disappearing fugitives."

"Let's get him locked up and worry about the logistics later. He must have weaknesses," Laura said.

The cops marched Peter away with his hands cuffed behind him. The crowd silently parted for them, and once they'd passed, the gossip and whispers started. Laura and Charlie ignored them, concentrating on controlling their captive.

The man slumped and let them haul him toward the police station. Saber and Leo caught up with them and flanked Isabella while the furious whispers grew louder. Some of the crowd were braver than others and flung questions at them. Everyone ignored the nosy interest, and when they rounded the corner, the noise reduced. The fire engine driver tooted the horn, and the crowd cheered.

They'd almost reached the police station when Peter's entire body jerked. He popped free of his cuffs and disappeared.

"Damn it!" Laura cursed.

"There he is," Isabella said. "At the end of the road."

Peter glanced over his shoulder and staggered several steps before righting himself. They sprinted after him, and he ran, lurching off balance. It was painfully easy to catch him, and when they did, he was even paler, his skin almost translucent.

Laura gripped Peter's arm while Charlie retrieved their handcuffs.

"You might as well let me go," Peter taunted. "I'm only going to keep popping out of the handcuffs."

"Not if we drug you," Charlie snapped. "I'll call Gavin."

"Excellent idea," Laura approved. "We'll keep him drugged until he gets to Australia, and then he's someone else's problem."

"I'll come back and take Kian. He belongs with me. I'm his uncle," Peter snapped, breathing hard.

Isabella sneered. He was in no condition to escape, and it was bravado talking on his part. It was easy to see that each time he teleported, he lost energy. It was why he traveled around in a rental car. They just needed to figure out how to keep him contained.

Isabella spotted movement from the far end of the street and only relaxed when she recognized Henry sliding through the shadows. Gerard slinked at his side, his inky black coat blending with the darkness. They were going to get this guy. She was positive it was him who'd murdered Jaycee.

"Why do you want Kian?" she demanded. "You've never shown an interest in him before. Jaycee never mentioned you, and we've been friends for a long time. How do I know you're even Jaycee's brother? We only have your word for it."

"Jaycee was a bitch. She thought she was too good for her real family."

Her uncanny skills had made her sought after by those searching for people and artifacts. "She wanted better for herself and her son. Why would she waste time on a screw-up like you?"

"I'm not a screw-up!" Peter screamed. "I showed her. She's dead, and I have her son."

Isabella opened her mouth to blast him, and he popped out again.

"Damn it," Laura snapped.

"There he is," Charlie shouted, pointed farther along the street at the hunched man who appeared years older than his actual age as he dragged his feet.

The teleporting was sapping his energy big time, but the man had determination. She'd give him that.

Isabella took off at a sprint. Peter glanced over his shoulder, saw her coming, and plucked a gun out of his pocket. He fired, and everyone scrambled for cover.

"Did you do a weapon check?" Isabella demanded.

"I patted him down and didn't locate a gun," Laura said, her voice even.

"Sorry," Isabella muttered. "That wasn't nice of me. You're good at your job."

"We're operating in unfamiliar territory here," Laura said. "We work together to catch him again, then we'll decide his fate."

Isabella had a suggestion, but she didn't think she should tell Laura. The only way to stop Peter was for him to die.

"We'll drive him down the street," Saber said. "Gerard and Henry will stop him from escaping unless he has the energy to vanish again."

"Plan," Charlie said. He and Laura exchanged a glance, and they must've agreed. Catching him now, with most focused on the Christmas festivities in the main street, would work best.

"Don't come any closer," Peter shouted. "I'll shoot. This gun is a new weapon. It will put an enormous hole in you."

"Threatening police officers is a felony charge. Give yourself up before you make this entire situation worse," Laura warned.

"Stay back!" Peter's hand trembled, and the weapon shook too much to shoot with accuracy.

Without warning, a dull *splat-splat* sounded, and a large hole appeared in the building before them.

"Holy fuck," Laura muttered. "That's a big-arse hole."

"We need a better plan," Charlie murmured.

"Our best plan is to keep drifting forward," Leo said calmly. "He's spooked. His hands and legs are trembling too much for him to shoot straight."

"And if he flukes a skilled shot?" Laura asked, heavy on the irony.

"He can't shoot all of us. Gerard and Henry are almost in position. He hasn't sensed their presence because he's focused on us. We need to keep his attention," Isabella said. "Laura, you and Charlie talk to him. Treat him like a victim you need to talk off a ledge. Claim his focus and push him."

"And if he shoots?" Laura snapped.

"Stay where you are now. We're close enough for him to hear. We have to get him under control before an innocent walks down this street. It won't be long before the fair ends," Isabella warned.

"She's right," Charlie said.

"Unfortunately, I agree. Although, what we're going to do with him when we catch him is another big-arse problem," Laura whispered.

"I'll post on the shifter community board," Saber said. "Another town might've faced the same problem. Let's grab him first, then deal with the next stage." Saber glanced at her and Leo, all three communicating with a single glance.

The only way to keep Kian and the feline community safe.

MY PRECIOUS GIFT

Peter wasn't leaving here alive.

Chapter 20

So Much Paperwork

"Surrender," Laura shouted. "That's the only way this situation will resolve itself."

"You s-should give up," Peter replied, his voice strained. "You can't keep me contained. Give me Kian, and I'll leave."

"He's a little boy," Charlie said. "He has lost his mother and deserves peace. A family. He has that here in Middlemarch, and it's what his mother wanted. Do you have a wife? How will you provide for him?"

"Why did you murder his mother? Your sister?" Laura demanded. "You're not doing this out of the goodness of your heart. Do you intend to sell him?"

Peter ignored the question.

"Keep talking. Ask him again why he wants Kian," Isabella whispered to Laura as she edged past.

Laura glared at Isabella. "Don't shoot him."

"How can we keep Kian and Middlemarch residents safe if he can pop in and out at will? He's no dummy. He'll learn there are more children like Kian in Middlemarch. Money is at the bottom of this. He has a buyer for Kian. That's why he murdered Jaycee. Peter wants the big payoff."

Laura stared at Isabella for a moment, her face pale in the growing darkness. In the distance, the voices raised in a harmonic rendition of 'Silent Night.'

While Charlie and Laura kept Peter talking, the rest of them crept closer, using the cars parked on the streets as cover. Isabella couldn't see Gerard and Henry, but they must be close. Yes, there they were—directly behind Peter. She made eye contact and gave a brief nod.

Given his current physical weakness, she doubted he'd blink out again, but if he found the power to do that, she'd shoot him first. Isabella pulled a gun from her thigh holster, hidden by her long shorts. She wasn't worried about hitting Henry or Gerard because she continually practiced her weapon skills, even though she'd officially retired.

"How much money are you getting for Kian, Peter?" Laura shouted. "What is the price on one boy's head?"

Peter laughed. "God, you have no idea. You wouldn't believe me if I told you."

"How much money, Peter?"

"Five million," he spat.

"And if you don't turn up with the boy?" Charlie shouted. "What will happen then?"

"I'll die," Peter snapped. "Not happening. I might not have Kian right now, but I will nab him."

Isabella had heard enough. She shot him in the right shoulder, and as she hoped, he dropped his weapon. It clattered to the ground, and Gerard and Henry leaped at him.

A loud, panicked scream rent the air. Henry gripped his arm and bit down. Gerard grasped his free arm, and another cry rang out because they weren't gentle.

Laura gingerly kicked his weapon out of reach. Saber secured it while Isabella and Leo raced forward, their otherness allowing them greater speed than Laura.

"Give me your gun," Leo demanded of Isabella.

His tone was something she'd never heard from him. Leo was typically easygoing and full of smiles.

She handed over the weapon, and Leo aimed it at Peter and fired.

Everyone froze. The boom of the shot had Isabella's ears ringing, and it echoed in the confines of the street, ricocheting between the brick and wooden buildings. Gerard and Henry released Peter, and he groaned.

"Leo, put the gun down," Laura said in a slow, careful voice.

Peter pushed up to a seated position with a tortured groan, and Leo fired again, his face hard. This time, Peter stayed down.

Again, no one moved, shocked by Leo's actions.

"Give me the gun," Isabella whispered.

Henry nudged the body with his nose and glanced at Saber. Leo's brother stalked over to Peter and checked his pulse.

"He's dead," Saber announced.

"What are we going to do now?" Laura demanded. "I can't cover this up."

"You won't have to," Isabella said. "We all saw the same thing. He kidnapped Kian and didn't intend to back down. We know he murdered Jaycee before he came for Kian. Peter died trying to kidnap Kian. That's the story we tell the authorities."

"Laura," Saber said, "he'd seen Gerard's and Henry's animal forms. It was only a matter of time before he clicked Middlemarch is a shifter community, and we would've faced real trouble. His death is the best result any of us could hope for, and it will keep everyone safe."

"He needed to pay for Jaycee's death." Leo's voice was harsh. "It was our right to take his life and revenge for Kian. The kid should grow up knowing his mother loved him to the end and fought to keep him safe from her brother."

"But the paperwork," Laura complained.

"Liaise with the detective in Melbourne," Saber said. "Let's get Gavin to sign off on his death. Then you contact the detective, and we can call it a job well done. Hopefully, we'll gain more information when we search his rental car and wherever he was staying. I got the impression he'd sold Kian to someone. It could've been for experimentation or a private zoo. We might never discover Peter's true plans for Kian, but if it helps to save others, it will be worth it. At the least, we can alert other shifters and perhaps disrupt the traffic of shifters."

Laura pulled a face. "But the paperwork."

"They're right," Charlie said to his colleague. "We couldn't keep him contained, not with the way he kept disappearing. This was the best alternative."

Gavin strode around the corner, his medical bag in hand, and Saber strolled to meet the local shifter doctor and vet. They had a quick discussion before Gavin approached.

"So much paperwork," Laura muttered with a shake of her head. "Okay." She turned to Isabella and Leo. "Leave before I change my mind. Charlie and I will contact the Melbourne detective and tell him we've caught his murderer."

"Thank you," Isabella said.

Leo nodded at them and took her arm. Isabella heard Saber ask if they needed help, and when Laura answered in the negative, he stalked after Leo and her and fell into step.

"You okay, bro?" Saber asked.

Exactly what Isabella wanted to know. Leo's actions hadn't been typical. If anyone killed the man, it should've been her since she already had hundreds of deaths to her name. Nothing she boasted about because taking a life was a serious matter and an act she never did lightly. Peter had deserved to die.

"The world is improved without him in it," Leo said, his voice hard and carrying none of his usual humor.

Isabella frowned and reached for Leo's hand. She wove their fingers together and squeezed hard. Relief poured through her when Leo responded with faint pressure against her digits.

"I agree," Saber said. "If you hadn't killed him, I would've done it myself. Laura can posture all she wants about the law and paperwork, but the truth is he would've escaped, would've kept coming at us. If he'd learned our kids are shifters but haven't shifted yet, that Kian was unusual in our world, his attack would never cease. If he were sourcing Kian for a medical lab, learning he had a pool of children for the scientists to study would've been hard for him to resist. The man killed his sister to get to Kian. That shows he was desperate or had no scruples." Saber paused. "Probably both," he decided. "No guilt. You did the right thing. Laura and Charlie will reach the same decision once they consider Peter's death. Their feline mates will help them understand our point of view."

Leo nodded, and Isabella sent a thankful glance to Saber. He winked at her, but she truly was grateful. Leo respected Saber's opinion and his support meant everything.

"I'll call Emily," Saber said when they turned onto the main street. "It'll be difficult finding them in this crowd."

"I told them to stay at Caroline's dress stall," Isabella said.

"I'll call, anyway. It looks as if the night's events are winding down. Hey, Emily," Saber broke off their conversation to speak to his mate. "Where are you?"

"Is everything okay?" she asked, her anxiety bleeding through with a shake to her words.

"We're safe and have everything settled," Saber said. "We're on our way to meet you."

"Come to the café," Emily said. "It became difficult to keep the kids confined, and since the night's activities were ending, we bribed them with ice cream and cake."

"Smart," Saber said. "We'll be there in ten minutes."

It was chaos when they knocked on the rear café door. Isabella could hear the kids' thumps as they ran around the interior and their shrieks of laughter and excitement.

Emily scrutinized them as she ushered them inside, and her bright smile faded. "Are you positive everything is okay?"

"Yes," Isabella spoke since Leo had gone silent. It was best if they collected Kian and drove home. Isabella had the perfect method to keep Leo busy. Her smile grew. Two ways, actually. "We'll grab Kian and head home. What a hell of a night. Thanks for watching Kian for us."

"Any time," Emily said. "He's a great kid, and his presence keeps my girls from fighting with each other. He's welcome anytime."

"A peacemaker," Isabella said, brightening. "We could do with harmony after tonight."

"He's gone?" Emily murmured.

"He's dead," Leo corrected. "He won't bother any of us ever again."

They still needed to delve into his history and learn if anyone might search for him, but that research could wait until tomorrow. Isabella was confident with their combined resources, they'd all keep safe.

Kian emerged from the group of children and trotted over to her and Leo. He stopped a few steps away from them, his nostrils flaring as he drew in scents. He'd smell Peter on them. Perhaps blood.

Isabella hesitated, dithering uncharacteristically over what to say.

"Peter has gone," Leo said. "He won't ever come back."

Kian scrutinized them before focusing on Leo. Despite his young age, Isabella was positive he understood why Peter would never return. He crossed the short distance between them and hugged Leo's leg.

"Home time?" Isabella asked.

Kian waved at the children before smiling at Emily. "Thank you," he said.

Emily's mouth fell open, but she recovered fast and bent to give Kian a quick hug. "You are welcome."

"Mr. Saber," Kian said and gave a surprising nod toward a bemused Saber.

Isabella couldn't have been more proud. "Let's go home."

· ♥ · ♥ · ♥ · ♥ · ♥ ·

Leo drove Isabella and Kian home, mind and body feeling years older than when they'd left home. He'd killed Peter because the man had threatened his family, and Leo had acted accordingly. Not a single regret popped out to niggle him. Not yet, at any rate.

When they arrived home, Leo parked the car. "I might do a quick security check," he told Isabella.

"I'll get Kian into bed. We have an important assignment tonight."

Leo frowned, but Isabella wasn't any more forthcoming. He shrugged and strode around the corner of the house. The security scan helped him walk off the remaining angst in body and soul, the edginess retreating until only fatigue remained.

How the hell did Isabella deal with the memories? He hadn't understood the gravity of taking a life, and now the second-guessing powered through his mind. He kept returning to the same conclusion.

One of them had needed to take out Peter. Laura and Charlie would've imprisoned him, giving the man, or whatever the hell he'd been, the opportunity of an easy escape.

Now Kian was safe. His family wasn't in danger.

That was all that mattered.

Leo stalked inside and locked up before going in search of Isabella. She was in Kian's bedroom and reading him more of the book about a lion getting a haircut. Judging by Kian's drooping eyes, it wouldn't take long before the boy fell asleep.

"How about an Irish coffee?" she suggested. "Or just a whisky."

"I'll be in the kitchen," Leo said.

Isabella gave him a chin lift and continued reading.

Leo watched them for a moment. Kian looked so tiny in the bed, even though his large paws indicated he'd grow to a decent size. Poor kid had gone through so much, losing a father, grandparents, and mother before his deranged uncle sought to profit from him. No, the man was better off dead. Leo shoved away his discomfort and the faint rumblings of guilt and ambled to the kitchen.

Isabella appeared, her arms laden with shopping bags and rolls of festive wrapping paper. "There are more," she said, her cheeks pink with an excitement he rarely witnessed in his mate.

She made four more trips, and soon their immaculate kitchen table looked like an explosion of Christmas with wrapping paper, tape, colored ribbons, Christmas stockings, and tiny gift cards.

"What's all this?" Leo asked.

"Tomasine and Emily were having trouble with their kids nosing through cupboards and drawers. They couldn't find a place to hide their gifts, so I suggested giving them to me. I told them we'd deliver the stockings to their houses on Christmas Eve after the kids had gone to bed."

"Which gift goes to which child?" Leo asked, staring at the bags.

"They have labeled everything. I figured you might have trouble sleeping tonight. Now is the perfect time for our task. I have a stocking for Kian too."

"All right." Leo smiled because his clever mate had discovered the perfect way to shunt them back into the Christmas spirit. "How long will it take us?"

"An hour. The stocking stuffing part is straightforward. Emily and Tomasine have given us lists as well."

"What about the fresh orange?" Leo asked. "Our parents always used to put an orange in our Christmas stockings."

"I've never had one," Isabella said. "Until I started spending Christmas with your family, I didn't understand the reasoning behind a Christmas stocking and Santa Claus."

"You never told me," Leo said.

Isabella shrugged. "I don't like to dwell on the past. The present and the future with you and Kian. That's what I want."

"Sounds perfect to me," Leo said, deciding at that moment to get Isabella an embroidered stocking this year. An orange. Some chocolate. A new pair of earrings and lacy lingerie. Emily and Tomasine would help him once he told them Isabella had never experienced this tradition. "We should have Christmas music." He found a radio station playing Christmas tunes, and soon festive background music flowed into the kitchen.

Isabella had been right. Once they found a system, it didn't take long to fill the stockings. They chatted over the task about the coming few days and sipped an excellent Scottish whisky. Leo relaxed and became more himself, the remaining tension flowing from his muscles.

"These we wrap," Isabella said, gesturing at the other bags. "Why don't we save these until tomorrow night?"

"Plan," Leo said. "Thank you, Isabella. This was fun and the distraction I needed."

Her violet eyes blazed with genuine love as she turned to him with a wide smile. "You're my mate. I'd do anything for you."

Chapter 21

Oranges and a Laptop

It was midnight by the time they finished and fell into bed.

"Come here," Leo said, drawing his naked, enticing mate into his arms. "I want to make love to my wife."

"That could be fun," Isabella said. "Although we need to stay quiet because we have a child now."

"I can be quiet, but can you?"

"You know those rumors about me being an assassin?"

"Yes," Leo said, his heart beating faster because *that* man's face slid into his mind. He shoved him right back out. *No regrets.* Not one damn regret.

"Everyone whispered of me—the silent assassin."

"Really?"

Isabella burst out laughing. "No. You should see your face."

That's when Leo realized something else. His wife didn't intend to tiptoe around this death, nor did she plan to baby him, which was the best way. "I'm not sorry I killed him. I'd do it again."

"Exactly right," Isabella said. "If you hadn't, I would've done the deed. Jaycee counted on us to keep Kian safe, and that's what we did. Now kiss me."

Leo embraced his love and kissed her. Their kiss started gently. Leo cupped her head, her blonde hair soft beneath his palm, and took the kiss deeper, sliding his tongue into her mouth and tipping the exchange into passion. When their lips parted, they were both breathing hard. Their lovemaking took on a dreamlike quality with more kisses, gliding caresses, and lingering pleasure. Leo pushed into Isabella's warmth, his mouth catching her groan.

It was romantic and reaffirmed their love.

It was togetherness.

Perfect togetherness.

Isabella's generous love tamped down his guilt, his regret.

He withdrew and surged into her again, kissing her at the same time. Isabella clutched his shoulders and shuddered an instant before she climaxed. Leo pushed into her again, the tiny fluttering of her pussy driving him over the edge. He stilled, their breaths audible and pulses racing.

"I love you, Isabella," Leo said.

"Leo," she whispered, pressing her forehead against his, "I love you too." She smiled. "It was fun doing the stockings. Do you think Kian will enjoy his gifts?"

Leo separated their bodies and drew her back into his arms. "I think we'll enjoy him exploring the contents as much as he relishes digging everything out of his stocking."

"Yeah," Isabella said. "I'll buy oranges tomorrow."

"Why don't you let me do the orange shopping?"

"Deal," Isabella said and yawned.

Leo closed his eyes, breathing in Isabella's scent. *His brave, gorgeous mate.* He fell asleep with a smile on his face.

But he woke with a scowl when something bounced on his belly. He growled without opening his eyes, delighting in Isabella's giggle. "Is it morning already?"

"Yeah, and Kian is wide awake. Judging by the rumble of his belly, he's hungry."

Leo pried his eyes open and almost smiled when he found Kian's furry face pressed close to his. His big blue eyes looked anxious, and he released a tiny mew. His tummy gurgled.

"Kian, close your eyes," Isabella ordered.

The boy obeyed instantly, dropping to his belly and resting his head on his paws. Isabella slipped from the bed and pulled on her clothes before heading to the kitchen. An instant later, Leo heard the coffee machine gurgle.

"Good boy," Leo said. "Would you like to visit the vineyard with me today? After that, you can help me buy Isabella a secret Christmas present. Would you be able to help me with that?"

Kian licked Leo's hand.

"That's a yes," Leo said with a chuckle. "You can open your eyes now." Leo climbed out of bed. Once dressed, he turned to Kian and ruffled his fur. "Let's get you ready for the day."

When Leo led Kian into the kitchen—in his two-legged form now—Isabella had bacon cooking.

"That smells fantastic. Kian and I have decided he's coming with me today. We're visiting the vineyard, then we're off to Queenstown and ice cream on the lakefront. Did you want us to pick up anything for you?"

"Can you do the grocery shopping? I can give you a list, then I won't need to go tomorrow. Emily deserves a break from the café." Isabella served the bacon and scrambled eggs.

A knock sounded as she placed the plates in front of Kian and Leo.

"I'll get it." Leo disappeared from the kitchen.

Voices drifted in from the doorway, and Isabella frowned because she didn't recognize their callers.

"Eat your breakfast, Kian," Isabella murmured when Kian tilted his head to listen.

His tiny *humph* of disapproval made Isabella want to laugh.

"Come in," she heard Leo say. "We're eating breakfast in the kitchen."

An instant later, Isabella stiffened. "What the hell?"

"Suzie and Edwina have something to tell us," Leo said. "Coffee?"

Isabella couldn't muffle her snort, and the girls jumped.

"We didn't have to come," Edwina snapped, her hackles rising.

"No, we're pleased you're here," Leo said. "Please tell Isabella what you told me."

The girls shared a glance before turning to Isabella.

"We decided to rent out the farm cottages, and Peter rang and booked. He paid extra for privacy and told us he was enjoying the solitude and rest after working on a tough assignment at his job. He told us he is the director of a large company," Edwina said.

"Peter seemed decent, but Gran told us what he'd done and how he'd intended to sell Kian. We had to speak with you." Suzie's voice trembled, and there was no doubting her sincerity.

"Suzie and I started thinking since we remembered he had a briefcase with him. He didn't take it to the café when we met him for coffee." She lifted the large shopping bag she carried. "We thought you should have it first before the human police." Edwina paused and lifted her chin. "I want to apologize for my bitchiness. My parents—Suzie's too—are refusing to let us attend university in Wellington. Our grandmothers told them we should leave school at the end of this year and get a job in Dunedin. They expect us to live in Middlemarch."

Suzie straightened. "None of this explanation excuses our behavior, but we wanted to tell you why we've been angry. Furious. We'd hoped they'd give in, but if anything, our actions have made the situation worse."

"Take a seat," Leo said. "What field of study interests you? Could you not do the same course at Otago University?"

"We want to study music," Suzie said. "Only the university in Wellington offers the course. Gran—both our grans—think music is a waste of time. They made sure we studied courses to equip us to be secretaries and office managers. It feels as if we're being punished, so we've reacted badly. I'm so sorry for our part in Peter's kidnapping of Kian. If we'd known his plan, we'd have come clean sooner."

Isabella placed mugs of coffee in front of both girls. "Please sit."

"I'll call Saber," Leo said.

Isabella glanced at Edwina and Suzie, a gush of sympathy filling her. Their grandmothers were strong, dominant women, and it couldn't be easy for teens wanting to experience the world. It had taken guts on their part to come and apologize. To explain. "Leo, why don't you call London and ask her if she'd come as well?"

"Why?" Edwina demanded.

"London and Saber are the youngest members of the Feline Council and will be most sympathetic to your situation," Isabella said. "Are other shifter teens facing the same problem? If you think of anyone, have them contact London or Saber, and they can go to bat for all of you because you're right. You shouldn't have to give up your dreams. Your grandmothers are wrong to keep you confined in Middlemarch. You understand the need to keep your feline secret, and they need to let you experience life and the freedoms you deserve."

Edwina blinked. Suzie stared.

"What?" Isabella barked. "I was young once. I had dreams. Right, hand over the laptop."

The bag rustled as Edwina passed it to Isabella.

"Saber is on his way," Leo said, stepping back into the kitchen. "London too." He checked his watch. "Kian and I need to get going. Do you want me to put off my meeting?"

Isabella shook her head. "No, you go. Make sure the staff don't give Kian too many sweets. I've noticed they make him more hyper than normal."

"Oh. Okay," Leo said, picking up his breakfast plate and Kian's. He took them over to the sink and rinsed them before stacking them in the dishwasher.

"My father would never wash a dish," Edwina whispered to Isabella, her eyes as round as the face of her wristwatch. "My grandfather either."

"We share the household tasks and everything else," Leo said, overhearing the softly spoken words without difficulty. "My brothers and our male friends do the same."

Suzie and Edwina shared a speaking glance. "We need a man like that. We can't live the lives our grandmothers envision for us," Suzie said.

Isabella powered up the laptop and noted it was password protected. The computer seemed fairly new, so she restarted it. The second time, she hit a key that took her to a *recover your account* page. After that, it was simple to change the password and gain entry to the laptop's contents. Fortunately, this was the extent of his security. A quick scan of his documents and email gave Isabella the details she wanted.

"Anything?" Leo asked. He held Kian's hand and plucked the keys for his truck off the counter. He stalked over to Isabella and bent to kiss her cheek.

She grinned up at him. "Everything we need to take down these people."

"Saber has arrived," Leo said. "Oh, London is with him. I'll let them in. Kian and I will return this afternoon. We'll bring something for dinner. Have you written your shopping list?"

"I'll text it to you in a bit," Isabella said and lifted her hand in a wave at Kian.

The boy waved before leaving the house. *Her two men.* Isabella grinned, taking pleasure at the thought before greeting her visitors.

"Saber, London, come on in. Coffee or tea?"

"I've got it," Edwina said. "Ah, coffee capsules." She set to work.

"Saber, do you have contacts in Europe?" Isabella asked. "I do, but I'd prefer not to use them if possible."

Saber took the seat beside Isabella. "What have you got?"

"The name of the man who intended to buy Kian for five million," Isabella said, her anger bleeding through in her words.

Saber turned to Edwina and Suzie. "Everything you hear this morning goes no further. This is council business, and I'm assuming Isabella has a reason for your presence."

"We know how to keep our mouths shut," Edwina said with quiet dignity.

"We will not speak to anyone about this, apart from you, London, and Isabella," Suzie said with sincerity.

"Edwina and Suzie knew where Peter was staying, and they brought the laptop and his other papers to us," Isabella said. Taking in Saber's raised eyebrows, she added, "They also gave Leo and I an explanation of why they've been pains in the butt and created town-wide problems."

"Talk," Saber ordered. "Tell me everything."

Both girls spoke at once.

"You first," Saber said, pointing at Suzie.

Isabella winked at London and returned to checking the laptop contents. That done, she went through the papers Suzie and Edwina had collected. Mainly receipts, but they offered a picture of where he'd been. She slowed when she came to several receipts from Melbourne businesses. This proved Peter had been in Melbourne and in the hospice's region during Jaycee's murder. Some of them were time-stamped. She snapped a photo of the receipts. They couldn't tell the detective the entire story, but a partial truth would give him and his men closure.

Isabella finished before Saber concluded his chat with Edwina and Suzie. London listened and tossed in a question now and then. Isabella observed surreptitiously while watching Saber's expression. He gave away little, but she'd learned to read her brother-in-law after knowing him for several years.

Isabella cleared the dirty breakfast dishes and switched on the dishwasher before returning to her seat. She wanted to discuss the Kian matter with Saber before she called the detective.

"All right," Saber said finally. "I want you to promise me you will behave over the Christmas vacation. Emily needs someone extra to work in the café. It won't be glamorous. You'll be clearing tables and greeting customers. I'll ask around and find something else, so you both have a job. Meanwhile, behave and let me and London fashion a plan. You're right. You shouldn't have to stay in Middlemarch for the rest of your lives. I stayed because of my brothers, and I had land and enjoyed farming. Don't mention this meeting to anyone. Wait until we have a viable plan. Okay?"

Isabella caught Edwina's surprise and saw it echoed in Suzie.

"Thank you," Suzie said. "I'd love to have a job to fill in time."

"Me too," Edwina said. "There isn't much to do in Middlemarch. Sitting around makes me think about everything out of my reach." She shrugged and stared down at her hands. "Boredom makes me misbehave. I'll try to do better."

"We both will," Suzie said. "Just knowing you listened to us and have offered us a job is huge. Thank you."

"All right. Emily will expect one of you in an hour," Saber said. "If one of you has a vehicle or has a friend in Queenstown, I can probably sort out a restaurant job."

The teens exchanged a glance. "I have an aunt who lives in Queenstown," Suzie said. "I'm sure she wouldn't mind me staying with her, and my parents would approve if it meant I had a holiday job."

"Done," Saber said. "Suzie, I'll call you later this afternoon."

The two girls left, leaving Isabella with London and Saber.

"I sort of feel sorry for them now," she said. "I caught them graffitiing in the town and reported them to Laura, but given the circumstances, I understand them acting out. How will you handle this?"

"A little research," London said, the sound of England simmering in her words. "We have a larger group of teenagers now, and if we're not careful, we'll lose them all."

"We'd be going backward. The town will end up with a shortage of marriageable women again." Saber grinned at London. "That's our starting point at the next meeting. We can mention the trouble we've had in town, how the kids require challenges, but we must nurture their dreams, otherwise we risk them never returning to Middlemarch once they become independent adults. Agnes and Valerie are behind this situation with their granddaughters. We need to remind them how they felt at the same age and what they're doing to their granddaughters by denying them the ability to chase their dreams." He rubbed his hands together. "This should be fun."

"I'm glad you think so," London said, her tone on the tart side. "They think I should side with them because I'm female. The truth—they've created this problem, and it's going to take time for them to admit this truth. Do you need me for anything else?"

"No, I want to talk to Isabella about Kian's situation," Saber said.

"I'll be off then. The Christmas fair went well last night. I had residents asking if we would hold it again next year," London said.

"Is Leo okay?" Saber asked as soon as they were alone. "He seemed his normal self, but it's hard to tell."

"We talked last night. This guy wouldn't have stopped. He would've kept coming for Kian, and there might've come a time when we couldn't beat him. He wouldn't have killed Kian because he was valuable in money terms, but Kian's safety remained an issue while Peter was alive. Judging by what I've found on his laptop, he owed money to loan sharks, and they were pushing for payment."

"You explained this to Leo?"

"Yes, he understands. He's protective of Kian. We both are because he's an awesome boy. We...we never thought we'd have a child in our lives, which makes Kian extra precious. He has burrowed into our hearts."

"Mine, too." Saber grinned—a wide and bright smile that made Isabella smile, too. "He doesn't say much, but he loves the outdoors."

"His father obviously spent time with him and trained him. He understands he can't shift when he's around people. Even though we've told him to ask first, he shifts at will when he's inside the house, but I figure he's a work in progress. Kian doesn't usually shift when he is with the other kids."

"My girls adore him," Saber said. "They talk enough to make up for his lack of prattle."

"I worry about him missing Jaycee. He's had so much to deal with recently. What if Leo and I fail?"

Saber chuckled. "I told Leo this a few days ago. I thought I had experience with kids. You've heard how I ended up in charge of my brothers. But having your own kids is different. No matter how much you prepare, there's a lot of on-job learning. You and Leo are doing a fantastic job. Kian was happy to head off with Leo this morning, but he's equally happy playing with the kids or doing farm chores with Felix and me. Parenting isn't easy. You learn as you go, and if something difficult crops up, you ask for advice. Emily and I learned from Tomasine and Felix. I've said it before, but I'll say it again. Hit up any of us for advice when you need it. We're here for you."

"Thank you."

"I mean it. No question is too stupid. Oh, and Mr. Google is your friend. And one more thing, Isabella. If Leo hadn't shot that bastard last night, I would've."

Chapter 22

Family

"Now remember," Leo said. "This is our secret. No telling Isabella what is inside. Okay?"

"Yes." Kian's blue gaze was earnest, and an air of suppressed excitement sizzled from him.

Leo had also organized other items during their trip, and he couldn't wait to give them to Kian and Isabella.

Leo and Kian tromped into the house, laden with groceries and secret shopping.

"How about a picnic dinner at the river and a swim afterward?" Isabella asked. "It's such a hot day, I thought it might be refreshing to swim. I'll paddle," she added since her shifter half didn't cope well with cold river dips.

"I'll put these in a safe place." Leo sent an exaggerated wink at Kian, and the boy grinned.

Isabella's heart stuttered, even as melancholy pulsed to the fore. She hated that Jaycee would never see her son grow into adulthood. Isabella pushed away the jagged emotions wanting to make memories for Kian, ones he'd recall with satisfaction and happiness.

Her two men shared a glance before turning back to her and nodding.

"Kian, do you want to help Isabella choose the food for dinner?" Leo asked.

He gave another enthusiastic nod and trotted after her while Leo lugged the bags of groceries into the kitchen and set them on the counter. "I'll be back in a minute to unpack the groceries."

"Several packages arrived from Australia," Isabella said to Leo.

Leo shot a glance at her, his brows rising. "From Melbourne?"

"Yes, with instructions not to open until 24th December. She had organization skills." Isabella sighed. "I wish things had turned out different."

"Me too, but we'll do our best with our cool little dude."

Isabella could read what else Leo was saying without verbalization. Jaycee had given them a precious gift. They might make mistakes, but they'd learn and grow with Kian. "This is an awesome opportunity for us. We hadn't planned on a child, but now we have one. We're blessed."

Leo's expression softened. "That's exactly how I feel. I was happy before, but Kian has turned us into a family."

Isabella crossed the distance between them, wrapped her arms around her mate. Groceries covered the counter, including treats for Kian and extra bananas. The book he'd read before breakfast sat near several cans of baked beans. She'd dumped a handful of yellow and blue construction bricks beside the book. Five pictures of various sizes stuck to the fridge door, the blast of color contrasting with the white cabinets. Their kitchen was no longer stylish and pristine, but it gave her even greater satisfaction.

"You're right. We're a family." Isabella's smile was wide as she beamed at him. She had extended family in the friends she'd made in Middlemarch. Every one of Leo's brothers would stand for her, as would their mates.

But now, she had a genuine family with Leo and Kian.

Sure, they'd have testing times, but she considered she'd won the lottery.

Chapter 23

Happiness

Kian climbed into bed around eight, and after the excitement of the angel party for Jaycee and opening one gift, it took him longer to settle. Tonight, instead of reading a book, Leo told Kian a childhood tale about him and his brothers not wanting to sleep on the night before Christmas.

"But you should sleep because otherwise, Santa will miss our house. He'll leave your presents at another kid's house. Maybe at Olivia's and Sophia's house, or Liam's or Bryce's. You wouldn't want them to get extras, would you?" Leo asked.

"Sylvie?" Kian asked, hugging his toy wolf.

"That's right," Leo said with a solemn nod. "Sylvie might score your gifts or another boy or girl who lives in Middlemarch."

Kian wrinkled his brow. "Mama?"

"She's happy in Heaven," Leo said. "She's probably watching you now after her angel party and *tsking*. Your mama might tell Santa to miss this house because you're not trying to sleep." Leo paused, fighting his amusement because he and his brothers had been terrors on Christmas Eve. Their parents had always had trouble getting them to stay in bed, let alone sleep. They'd tried bribery and other strategies. Sort of like he was doing. He'd need to ask Saber and Felix tomorrow how they'd managed.

As he watched, Kian's eyes closed. Leo waited, happy when the sleepiness stuck. Leo waited a fraction longer before he crept from the bedroom and joined his mate.

"That's Saber's vehicle," Isabella said. "He mentioned he'd be here around eight to pick up his girls' Christmas stockings."

"I'll let him in," Leo said.

He found Felix and Saber on his doorstep.

"Have you come for Christmas stockings?"

"Yep, I left Emily trying to get the girls to settle," Saber said.

Felix grimaced. "Our boys intend to stay awake to catch Santa in the act."

"Kian is asleep, but only just. It reminded me of the grief we gave our parents and later Uncle Herbert," Leo said. "It's payback. That's what it is."

Saber chuckled. "You're probably right. We deserve it. Hopefully, the kids will be asleep by the time we get home."

Leo winked at Isabella when he caught her listening. "Have a drink before you head out."

Leo hadn't realized he and Isabella were missing family-related moments because they hadn't had children. Now that they had a kid in the house, everything had changed. He herded his brothers and Isabella into the kitchen.

"Let's drink a toast," Leo said and reached for a bottle of Scottish whisky. He poured four glasses. "Let's toast to family and a special mention to Jaycee for bringing such joy to our lives."

"To family and Jaycee," they chorused.

· ♥ · ♥ · ♥ · ♥ · ♥ ·

Christmas Morning
Leo woke with a raspy tongue flicking over his cheek. Without opening his eyes, he said, "Kian, what did we tell you about asking one of us before you shift?"

The snow leopard backed up and shifted. He did a slight pout, so adorable Leo had to hide his grin.

"You were asleep," Kian said. "Couldn't ask when you were asleep."

"He's got you there," Isabella murmured without opening her eyes.

Leo glanced at his watch and saw it was seven. "I'll put on the coffee."

Isabella pushed up on her elbow. "I'll get up too."

"Grab a few more minutes," Leo said. "We have a busy day. I'll get Kian dressed and his breakfast ready."

"Are you sure?"

Leo leaned over and kissed her forehead. "Kian and I will keep busy for half an hour. Come on, Kian. You pick out clothes."

Leo yanked on his shorts and strode off to supervise Kian. Once the boy had dressed, they headed to the kitchen.

"What do you want for breakfast?" Leo asked and reached for the loaf of bread because he'd bet ten dollars the boy would want toast.

"Toast and honey," Kian said, licking his lips.

Leo laughed and loaded the bread into the toaster. With the coffee underway and Kian drinking a glass of milk, Leo sent a text to Henry.

MY PRECIOUS GIFT

We're awake if you have time to drop by with the item.

The return text came seconds later. **Be there in half an hour.**

Anticipation had Leo grinning. He couldn't wait to see Kian's reaction to the present he and Isabella had arranged for him.

Isabella wandered into the kitchen, and he handed her a mug of coffee.

"Kian is having toast and honey. Do you want toast too?"

"Do we still have strawberry jam?"

"We do." Leo had already reached for the jam. "So predictable."

"You can talk," Isabella grumbled. "Vegemite is your go-to."

"You don't fix something that isn't broken," Leo said, his tone solemn.

Isabella sipped her coffee, her eyes twinkling before she turned to Kian. "Did Santa visit last night? Have you checked?"

Kian blinked, his mouth falling open.

"Did you forget?" Leo teased.

"Before we check, this is a special one from your mama."

When Isabella produced a large package covered in bright red paper and candy canes, Kian's eyes grew wide.

"Mama?"

"Yes," Isabella said. "Let me take a photo for you to put in your album."

"Mama is in Heaven," Kian said, and he sounded sad.

Leo clasped Kian's hand, and Isabella squeezed the boy's shoulder as she moved his partially eaten toast and honey aside.

"Let's clean your hands, then you can open your mama's present. Can you guess what it is?" Isabella asked.

Kian sniffed the Christmas paper. He shook his head. "No."

"I don't know either," Isabella said. "You'd better hurry with those hands."

Kian jumped off his chair and hurried out of the kitchen. Moments later, the pipes rattled as he washed his hands.

"I didn't get around to telling you. Jaycee sent me what I think are birthday cards for every year until Kian turns twenty-one. She also included a key and details of land in Nepal. I see a trip in our near future."

"Everything about this situation punches me in the gut," Leo murmured. "Jaycee loved her boy so much. Her love shows in her preparations for his future. There must've been times when fatigue and the sickness attacked her, yet she held it together and planned everything. Many kids don't have that emotional support and love. We need to make sure he knows."

"We're going to love him and nurture him and make Kian realize how special his mother was," Isabella said in a thick voice.

"The angel party last night was the perfect start," Leo said. "The other kids enjoyed it too and did you see the expression in Kian when Sylvie told him his parents were a handsome couple? His chest puffed out, and I thought he might burst with pride."

Running footsteps heralded Kian's return.

"Clean," he announced, holding up his hands.

"Wet," Leo retorted and reached over to grab a paper towel.

Once his hands were dry, Isabella nodded at the brightly colored package. "Why don't you open that and see what your mama gave you?"

Kian ripped the parcel open with gusto. "*Ooh!*" he said on finding the paints and colored pencils, the crayons, and coloring books. The plain paper for sketching.

Someone knocked on the door.

"I'll get it," Leo said, before mouthing "Henry" at Isabella.

She nodded and distracted Kian with questions. "What will you draw first?"

"Wolf," Kian said after scrunching his brow.

"Of course you will." Kian adored Henry, and it was a wonder he hadn't scented his favorite person yet. He refused to sleep without his stuffed wolf and made a beeline for Henry if he spotted him.

"Isabella," Leo called from the lounge. Her signal to get Kian there.

"Kian, do you know what we forgot to do?" she asked.

"No," he replied after a while.

"We haven't checked in the lounge to see if Santa left you anything in your Christmas stocking."

His blue eyes widened.

"Should we go now?"

"Yes." Excitement filled his voice, and he scrambled off his chair, leaving his new art equipment on the table.

Just then, something barked.

Kian froze, his gaze darting to her. "Dog?"

Isabella's face strained under the wideness of her smile. "Why don't you check it out?"

MY PRECIOUS GIFT

Kian broke into a run and disappeared down the corridor. Isabella followed more slowly and heard his shriek seconds before she reached the lounge. She hustled and rounded the corner in time to see Kian drop to his knees in front of a husky puppy.

"Merry Christmas, Kian. Isabella and I thought you might like a puppy, and Henry had one ready to leave home. Will you look after her?"

"Yes," Kian shouted, his hands gentle as he ran them down the puppy's back. She was steel gray with a white belly, and her eyes were a similar blue to Kian's.

Boy and puppy regarded each other while Isabella fished out her phone to record the sweet moment.

"That seems settled," Henry said. "I have the puppy stuff in my truck."

"I'll help you unload," Leo said.

Isabella hunkered beside Kian. "You'll have to choose a name."

"Dog," Kian said.

Isabella laughed. "Because she will become your friend, she needs another name. A special one. You think about it today."

Kian hugged the puppy but gently, and she licked his face, making him giggle.

"You haven't checked out your stocking yet." Isabella turned toward the mantle where she and

Leo had hung Kian's stocking the previous night. She blinked and refocused, her mouth rounding as she stared at the second stocking that hung beside Kian's—the one with her name on it. She heard footsteps behind her and recognized the scent.

"Leo, I..." she trailed off, her throat tight. What was that thing Sylvie said when her feelings rose high? Oh. Yes. Right now, she experienced all the feels, and they threatened to burst from her chest.

"Why don't you and Kian start while I grab Henry a cup of coffee?" Leo asked.

"I can get my coffee." Henry stayed Leo with a firm hand to his shoulder. "You stay and watch. I'll be back soon."

Henry left with quiet footsteps that belied the size of the man.

"You—" Isabella broke off because she couldn't speak plainly in front of Kian. Her next words were a croak, and her throat grew so tight she didn't attempt to push any other words free.

"What is in your stocking, Kian? What has Santa left you?" Leo asked.

Henry returned and took a seat next to Leo on the couch. "Santa left nothing for me."

"You have puppies," Kian informed him.

Henry chuckled. "So do you now. You can come to visit me, and I'll teach you how to train her."

MY PRECIOUS GIFT

He finished his coffee and stood. "On that note, I'd better go."

"Thanks, Henry," Leo said.

Isabella hugged him goodbye, and an instant later, she heard Henry's vehicle depart.

Kian patted the puppy before he turned back to his stocking. He leaned closer to his red stocking and traced his finger over the green embroidery of his name. Then he sniffed the fabric and sneezed. He turned to Leo, his brows knit. "It smells the same as you."

"Santa arrived while I was locking up for the night. He told me he was in a hurry because he'd slept in late and was desperate to do his deliveries. I told him if he'd hand me your stocking contents, I'd place them inside for him. He was so pleased with my help he gave me a spare bag, so there was enough to fill a stocking for Isabella."

"I was lucky, and thank you for the explanation because I was wondering why my stocking smelled like my darling mate." Isabella held back her grin, delighted with Leo's explanation. Her heart expanded with love for this remarkable man, and everything seemed richer and more exciting with Kian's presence.

"I told Santa you'd never received a Christmas stocking. Santa told me it was an error because the elves were on to these things. When he tapped into his hand-held computer, he was shocked to learn I was correct. I think that was another reason he gave me the extra stocking."

Isabella grinned. The love behind Leo's gift made up for every disappointing year with her family. *Every single one.*

Kian pulled a large and shiny green ball from his stocking and issued a delighted hoot. He reached in and extracted a book containing stories about a wolf.

Entranced by his excitement, she wished Jaycee could see him. A sympathetic ache spread through her chest and disappointment for the loss her friend had borne. Kian was the best and most precious gift anyone had ever given her. She thought she'd been happy with Leo, but Kian had added an extra element, a richness, to their marriage, their lives. Isabella had always stood outside and stared through the window at the joy her friends experienced with their children. Oh, they'd face testing times along with the good, but what was life without a challenge?

"Isabella," Leo said, snapping a series of photos of Kian and the puppy. "Open your stocking. I want to take your photo."

MY PRECIOUS GIFT

Her smile started small, but it spread across her mouth until it became so broad her lips hurt. She reached into the stocking, and her figures came into contact with a rigid, square box. It was a royal blue box of the type that stored jewelry. She opened it to find a ring—a golden band encircled with emeralds. She glanced up at Leo.

"It's an eternity ring. It symbolizes never-ending love."

"Oh." She touched it with a delicate finger before taking it from the box and sliding it onto the same finger as her engagement and wedding rings. The stones reminded her of Leo's eyes. "It's perfect. Thank you."

Kian seemed to have the hang of unpacking his stocking now and eagerly showed Leo each new thing: a purple T-shirt with a wolf on the front, a candy cane, more art supplies, and a puzzle, also bearing a wolf picture. A book about snow leopards. He stroked the cover of this book.

Isabella found sexy lingerie, a box of her favorite chocolates, a Nalini Singh thriller, and last, she pulled out a fresh, fragrant orange.

Kian pulled an orange from the toe of his stocking and sniffed the fruit.

Isabella grinned. "I have an orange too. Have you eaten one before?"

Kian nodded, his eyes sparkling.

"Why don't we eat them for breakfast?"

Kian stood and carried his orange with him. "What about Dog?" he asked. "What will she have for breakfast?"

"Henry told me she has already had her breakfast. She won't eat again until dinner time," Leo said.

"We'll have to think of a name," Isabella said. "We can't go around shouting Dog. Everyone will laugh at us."

"What about a Christmassy name?" Leo asked. "Merry or Noel or Holly. What about one of those?"

"Holly," Kian said decisively. The puppy ran to him and jumped at his legs. Kian let out a delighted laugh.

Isabella shared a grin with Leo. "Holly, it is," she said. "That's a beautiful name."

She leaned over and kissed Kian's cheek. Leo kissed his other cheek, and they walked into the kitchen for breakfast.

"We have a family. We even have a dog," Isabella murmured.

Leo slipped his arm around her waist and tugged her against his side. "We *do* have a family, and I couldn't be happier. I have a gorgeous mate who constantly challenges me, a son who is delightful and mostly well-behaved, and now we have a

MY PRECIOUS GIFT

gorgeous puppy called Holly." Leo cupped her cheek and kissed her.

Isabella leaned into her mate and kissed him back, happy. *So happy.*

"Hungry," Kian said.

Isabella winked at her mate and strode to where Kian stood in the kitchen with his puppy. "We can't have that," she said. "I love you, Leo."

"Right back at you, sweetheart."

"This is gonna be a fantastic day," Isabella said.

"I think so too," Leo agreed.

And it was. The best Christmas ever.

Afterword

Want a peek at Leo, Isabella, and Kian's future?
Not quite ready to let Leo, Isabella, and Kian go?
Me neither.
Subscribe to my newsletter
at www.subscribepage.com/mypreciousgift_bonus
and receive *Kitty Singing*, a bonus story about their visit to Nepal.

Happy reading!
Shelley

About Author

USA Today bestselling author Shelley Munro lives in Auckland, the City of Sails, with her husband and a cheeky Jack Russell/mystery breed dog.

Typical New Zealanders, Shelley and her husband left home for their big OE soon after they married (translation of New Zealand speak - big overseas experience). A twelve-month-long adventure lengthened to six years of roaming the world. Enduring memories include being almost sat on by a mountain gorilla in Rwanda, lazing on white sandy beaches in India, whale watching in Alaska, searching for leprechauns in Ireland, and dealing with ghosts in an English pub.

While travel is still a big attraction, these days Shelley is most likely found in front of her computer following another love - that of writing stories of contemporary and paranormal romance and adventure. Other interests include watching rugby

SHELLEY MUNRO

(strictly for research purposes), cycling, playing croquet and the ukelele, and curling up with an enjoyable book.

Visit Shelley at her Website
www.shelleymunro.com

Join Shelley's Newsletter
www.shelleymunro.com/newsletter

Visit Shelley's Facebook page
www.facebook.com/ShelleyMunroAuthor

Follow Shelley at Bookbub
www.bookbub.com/authors/shelley-munro

Also By Shelley

Paranormal

Middlemarch Shifters
My Scarlet Woman
My Younger Lover
My Peeping Tom
My Assassin
My Estranged Lover
My Feline Protector
My Determined Suitor
My Cat Burglar
My Stray Cat
My Second Chance
My Plan B
My Cat Nap
My Romantic Tangle
My Blue Lady
My Twin Trouble
My Precious Gift

SHELLEY MUNRO

Middlemarch Gathering
My Highland Mate
My Highland Fling

Middlemarch Capture
Snared by Saber
Favored by Felix
Lost with Leo
Spellbound with Sly
Journey with Joe
Star-Crossed with Scarlett

Lightning Source UK Ltd.
Milton Keynes UK
UKHW030920180922
409053UK00001B/16